Dr. van Rijgen stirred. "Magnificent. Do you like our *Grote Kirk?*"

"It's breathtaking. I didn't know it was so old…all those years building it. I must get a book about it."

"I have several at home. You must borrow one."

Fran stood up and he stood up with her, which put her at an instant disadvantage for she had to look up to his face. "You want something, don't you?" she asked. "I mean…" She hesitated and blushed. "You don't—you aren't interested in me as—as a person, are you?"

"That, Francesca, is where you are mistaken. I should add that I have not fallen in love with you or any such foolishness, but as a person, yes, I am interested in you."

"Why?"

She spoke softly because there were people milling all round them now.

"At the proper time I will tell you…."

Romance readers around the world were sad to note the passing of **Betty Neels** in June 2001. Her career spanned thirty years, and she continued to write into her ninetieth year. To her millions of fans, Betty epitomized the romance writer, and yet she began writing almost by accident. She had retired from nursing, yet her inquiring mind still sought stimulation. Her new career was born when she heard a lady in her local library bemoaning the lack of good romance novels. Betty's first book, *Sister Peters in Amsterdam,* was published in 1969, and she eventually completed 134 books. Her novels offer a reassuring warmth that was very much a part of her own person-ality. She was a wonderful writer, and she will be greatly missed. Her spirit will live on in all her stories, including those yet to be published.

THE BEST *of*
BETTY NEELS

THE SECRET POOL

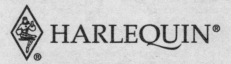

HARLEQUIN®

TORONTO • NEW YORK • LONDON
AMSTERDAM • PARIS • SYDNEY • HAMBURG
STOCKHOLM • ATHENS • TOKYO • MILAN • MADRID
PRAGUE • WARSAW • BUDAPEST • AUCKLAND

ISBN 0-373-51231-7

THE SECRET POOL

Copyright © 1986 by Betty Neels.

This edition published by arrangement with Harlequin Books S.A.

® and TM are trademarks of the publisher. Trademarks indicated with ® are registered in the United States Patent and Trademark Office, the Canadian Trade Marks Office and in other countries.

Visit us at www.eHarlequin.com

Printed in U.S.A.

CHAPTER ONE

THE early morning sun of a midsummer's day morning shone with warm cheerfulness on to the quiet countryside, the market town tucked neatly into the Cotswold hills and its numerous windows. These included those of the Cottage Hospital, a symbol of former days, fought for and triumphantly reprieved from the remorseless hand of authority, and proving its worth tenfold by never having an empty bed.

Inside the grey stone walls of this Victorian edifice, the day's work was already well advanced. Its thirty beds were divided between surgical and medical patients, with two beds for maternity cases who couldn't make it in time to Bristol or Bath, and one private ward used for any child too ill to move or anyone too ill to nurse in the wards. There was a small out patients' department, too, and a casualty room where the local GPs could be called to attend any accident. Small it might be, but it did yeoman service, easing the burden of patients on the big Bristol hospitals.

It was staffed by the local doctors, ably supported by Miss Hawkins, who still insisted on being called Matron, two ward sisters and their staff nurses, and four pupil nurses, sent from Bristol and Bath to gain experience. There was a night sister, too, and a handful of nursing aides, local ladies, whose kindness of heart and willingness to work hard when everyone else was fast asleep more than made up for their lack of nursing skills. Miss Hawkins was nearing retirement age, an old-fashioned martinet who had no intention of changing her ways. Until six months ago she had had the willing co-operation of Sister Coffin on the medical ward but that lady had retired and her place had been taken by a young staff nurse from the Bristol Royal Infirmary, who had accepted the post of sister in preference to a more prestigious one at her own hospital. It was agreed by everyone, even the grudging Miss Hawkins, that she had proved her ability and was worth her weight in gold. She had a happy knack of getting her patients better, coping with emergencies without fuss, carrying out the various doctors' orders faithfully, and lending a sympathetic ear to the young nurses' requests for a particular day off duty.

She sat at the desk in her office now, the sun gilding the mousy hair pinned neatly under her frilled cap, warming her ordinary face, escaping plainness only by virtue of a pair of fine hazel eyes, thickly lashed, and a gentle mouth. The desk was more or less covered by charts and a variety of forms and she had a pen in her hand, although just for the moment she was doing no work at all, her thoughts far away, if rather vague. She was normally a sensible girl, prepared to accept what life had to offer her and not expecting anything very exciting to happen. Indeed, the three elderly aunts with whom she lived had imbued her with this idea from an early age. They prided themselves on their honesty and plain spokenness and had pointed out on a number of occasions her lack of good looks and amusing conversation. They had done their best to dissuade her from training as a nurse, too, but she had been surprisingly stubborn; despite their certainty that she was too quiet, too shy with strangers, and lacking in self-assurance, she had gone to Bristol, done her training, and emerged at the end of it with flying colours: Gold Medallist of her year, the prospect of a ward sister's post in the not too distant future, and a circle of firm friends. The girls liked her because she listened to the details of their complicated love lives with sympathy. The young housemen liked her because she listened to them, too, about their fleeting love affairs and their dreams of being brilliant consultants. She sympathised with them when they failed their exams and rejoiced with them when they passed and, when on night duty, she was always a willing maker of hot cocoa when one or other of them had been hauled out of bed in the small hours.

But she had declined the ward offered her and had instead applied for and been appointed to the medical ward of the Cottage Hospital in her home town. All because her youngest aunt, Janet, had had a slight— very slight—heart attack and it had been impressed upon her by Aunt Kate and Aunt Polly that it was her duty to return home.

So she had come back to the small town and lived

out, going to and fro from her aunts' rambling old
house not ten minutes' walk from the hospital. And
because she was a good nurse and loved her work,
she had taken pride in changing the medical ward,
with patience and a good deal of tact, into the more
modern methods Sister Coffin had ignored. It had
been uphill work but she had managed it so well that
Matron considered that she had been the instigator of
change in the first place. If she regretted leaving her
training school and the splendid opportunities it had
offered her, she had never said so, but just now and
again she wondered if life would have been different
if she had taken the post at Bristol. She would have
kept her friends for a start and used her nursing talents
to their utmost; and who knew, perhaps one day she
might have met someone who would want to marry
her.

She stifled a sigh and looked up with a smile as
her staff nurse came in. Jenny Topps was a big girl,
always cheerful and amiable and with no wish to be
anything but a staff nurse. She was getting married in
a year's time to a rather silent and adoring young
farmer and her ambitions lay in being a good wife.
She said now,

'We're ready, Sister. There's time for a quick cup
of tea before Dr Beecham gets here. I've sent the little
nurses to coffee; Mrs Wills—the nursing auxilary—
is in the ward.'

'Good. Yes, let's have tea, then I'll go over to the
Women's Medical. It's quiet there and Staff can cope,

but I'll just take another look at Miss Prosser. Mr Owen's not responding to his antibiotic, is he? I'll see if Dr Beecham will change it. He might be better off at the Infirmary.' She took the mug of tea Jenny had fetched from the ward kitchen and sipped it.

'You must miss the Infirmary,' observed Jenny. 'It's pretty quiet here—bad chests and diabetics and the odd heart case…'

She studied Sister Manning's quiet face on the other side of the desk; she liked her and admired her and although she wasn't pretty she had a pretty name—Francesca.

'Well, yes, I do, but I do need to be near by my aunts…' She finished her tea, got to her feet and said, 'I'll be back in five minutes. Get the nurses to start making up that empty bed, will you? There is a diabetic coming in at two o'clock.'

The ward was quiet, the men waiting for the biweekly round from the consultant. Most of them were on the mend. Mr Owen worried her a little, and the new patient who had come in during the night, a suspected coronary, might spring something on them. She went slowly down the old-fashioned but cheerful ward, stopping for a word here and there and casting an eye on these two, and then went through the door into the women's side.

Here she was met by her second staff nurse, a small dark girl who like herself lived out.

'All ready for Dr Beecham?' asked Francesca.

'How's Miss Prosser? She was a bit cyanosed when I did the round this morning.'

'Still a bit blue. She's had some oxygen and she's quite bright and cheerful.'

They stood together and looked along the facing row of beds. It was a small ward with pretty curtains at the windows and round each bed, and plenty of flowers. Half the patients were up, sitting by their beds, knitting or reading or gossiping. Francesca walked slowly to Miss Prosser's bed and made small talk while she studied that lady. They had had her in before and she was by no means an easy patient; she would have to talk to Dr Beecham about her. She smiled and nodded at the other patients and went back to her office, tidied the top of her desk, and with a glance at the clock went back to the men's ward. Dr Beecham would be there at any moment now.

He came through the door within moments, a short stout man with a fringe of hair on a bald head and twinkling blue eyes. She had known him ever since she had begun her training; he had been one of the first lecturers she had had and as she became more senior he had occasionally explained some unusual case to her. She liked him and the smile which lighted up her face made it almost pretty.

He had someone with him. Not just Dr Stokes, who was the RMO; a tall man with massive shoulders, fair hair with a heavy sprinkling of grey and the good looks to turn any woman's head. Francesca sighed at the sight of him. She knew him, too: Dr van Rijgen,

a specialist in tropical diseases who had come to the
Infirmary at regular intervals to lecture the students.
He lived in Holland and worked there as far as she
knew, although he seemed equally at home in England. Years ago when she had begun her training she
had had the misfortune to drop off during one of his
lectures; even after all these years, she remembered
his cold voice, laced with sarcasm, very quietly re-
ducing her to a state bordering on hysteria. They had
encountered each other since then, of course, and she
had taken care never to allow her feelings to show,
and he for his part had never betrayed any recollec-
tion of that first unfortunate meeting. He eyed her
now with a kind of thoughtful amusement which
made her fume inwardly. But she replied suitably to
Dr Stokes and Dr Beecham and then bade him a
frosty good morning.

He had a deep slow voice. 'Good morning, Sister
Manning. I see that I must congratulate you since we
last met at the Infirmary.' He glanced round the ward,
half the size of those in a Bristol hospital. 'Hiding
your light under a bushel?'

She said in a voice which made his fine mouth
twitch, 'If I remember aright, sir, my light was a very
small one—a mere glimmer.'

He gave a crack of laughter. 'Oh, dear, you have
a long memory, Sister.'

'A useful thing in a nurse,' interpolated Dr Beecham cheerfully. 'What have you got for us today,
Fran?'

Dr Beecham prided himself on the good terms he enjoyed with the ward sisters and none of them minded that he addressed them by their Christian names when they were away from the patients.

'Nothing much, sir. There's Miss Prosser...' She didn't need to say more, they both knew that lady well enough. 'And Mr Owen who isn't so well. All the rest are making good progress.'

'Right, shall we see the ladies first? I want Dr van Rijgen to look at Mr Owen.'

The round wound its usual way, first through the women's ward and then the men's, to spend some time with Mr Owen; this time Dr van Rijgen did the examining. At length he straightened up. 'I agree with you, John,' he told Dr Beecham, 'he should be transferred to the Infirmary as soon as possible.'

He sat down on the side of the bed and addressed himself to Mr Owen. He explained very nicely, even Fran had to admit that, with a mixture of frankness and confidence which cheered the patient. 'And if Sister can arrange it, perhaps your wife would like to travel with you in the ambulance?'

He glanced at Dr Beecham who nodded and then turned his cold blue eyes upon Fran. 'Sister?'

'Mrs Owen lives close by, I am sure something can be arranged.'

They had coffee next, squashed in her office, discussing the round, pausing from time to time to alter drugs and give her instructions.

They had finished their coffee when Dr Beecham

reached for the phone. 'I'll warn the medical side, Litrik. What about his wife?'

Dr van Rijgen turned to Fran and found her eyes fixed on his face.

'Mrs Owen? Can you get her here so that we can have a word with her, Sister?'

He frowned impatiently when she didn't answer at once. She had never thought of him as having any name other than van Rijgen; the strange name Dr Beecham had said made him seem different, although she didn't know why. A strange name indeed, but quite nice sounding. She realised that he had spoken to her and flushed a little and the flush deepened when he repeated his question with impatience.

'Certainly, sir. I can telephone her, she lives less than five minutes' walk away.' She spoke crisply and thought how ill-tempered he was.

Dr Beecham had finished with the phone, and as she dialled a number he said, 'Right, Fran. We'll go along to X-Ray and look at those films. Litrik, will you talk to Mrs Owen?'

He patted her on the shoulder, said, 'See you later, Litrik,' and went away, taking Dr Stokes with him.

Mrs Owen was a sensible woman; she asked no unnecessary questions but said that she would be at the hospital in ten minutes. 'I'll not ask you any questions, Sister,' she finished, 'for I'm sure the Doctor will tell me all I want to know.'

Fran put down the receiver and glanced at Dr van Rijgen, sitting on the window ledge, contemplating the view. She had no intention of staying there under his unfriendly eye; she picked up the charts on the desk and got up.

'Don't go,' said Dr van Rijgen without turning round. 'However sensible Mrs Owen may be, she'll probably need a shoulder to cry on.'

He spoke coldly and she, normally a mild-tempered girl, allowed her tongue to voice her thoughts. She snapped, 'Yes, and that's something you wouldn't be prepared to offer.'

The look he gave her was like cold steel; she added, 'sir' and waited for his cold calm voice to utter something biting.

'It is a good thing that my self-esteem does not depend upon your good opinion of me,' said Dr van Rijgen softly. 'Would it be a good idea if we were to have a tray of tea? I have found that tea, to the English, soothes even the most unhappy breast. Come to that, the most savage one, too.'

Fran didn't look at him but went in a dignified way to the kitchen and asked Eddie, the ward maid, to lay up a tea tray.

''As 'is nibs taken a liking for it?' asked that elderly lady. 'Not like 'im, with 'is foreign ways.'

Fran explained, knowing that if she didn't Eddie was quite capable of finding out for herself.

'Give me 'arf a mo', Sister, and I'll bring in the tray. Three cups?'

'Well, yes, I suppose so. Mrs Owen won't want to sit and drink it by herself.'

She would rather not have gone back to the office but there was no reason why she shouldn't. Dr van Rijgen was still admiring the view and he didn't look at her when she sat down at her desk. Indeed, he didn't move until one of the nurses tapped on the door, put her head round it in response to Fran's voice and said that Mrs Owen was there.

Fran sat her down: a small plump woman, her round face so anxious. 'It's Jack, isn't it, Sister? He's not so well. I'm that worried…'

Fran poured the tea and said in a quiet way, 'Mr Owen has been seen by Dr Beecham and Dr van Rijgen this morning, Mrs Owen.' She handed the doctor a cup. 'Dr van Rijgen will explain how things are…'

He had got to his feet when Mrs Owen had been ushered in; now he sat on the edge of the desk, half turned away from Fran. He looked relaxed and unworried and Mrs Owen's troubled face cleared. His explanations were concise and offered with matter-of-fact sympathy; he neither pretended that there was much chance of Mr Owen recovering, nor did he paint too dark a picture of his future. 'We shall do what we can, Mrs Owen, that I can promise you,' he told her finally and Fran, listening, was aware that if she were in Mrs Owen's shoes she would believe him; what was more, she would trust him. Which, considering she didn't like the man, was something to be wondered at.

Dr van Rijgen went away presently, leaving Fran to give what comfort she could, and Mrs Owen, who had kept a stern hold on her feelings while he had been talking, broke down then and had a good cry, her grey head tucked comfortingly into Fran's shoulder. Presently she mopped her eyes and sat up. 'So sorry,' she said awkwardly, 'but it's a bit of a shock…'

Fran poured more tea and murmured in sympathy, and Mrs Owen went on, 'He's nice, isn't he? I'd trust him with my last breath. Funny, how you can feel he means what he says. Though I suppose he has to talk to lots of people like that.'

'Oh, yes, I'm sure he must. He's a very eminent doctor even though he's not English, but that doesn't mean that he doesn't understand your husband's case, Mrs Owen, and have every sympathy with you both.'

'And you, you're a kind girl too, Sister. My Jack thinks a lot of you.'

Fran made a comforting murmur and, since Mrs Owen was calm again, embarked on the business of ways and means. 'I still have to arrange things with the ambulance; it'll be some time tomorrow morning, quite early, if you could manage that? If you could come here? The ambulance will have to come back here, but I expect you'd like to stay for a bit and see Mr Owen settled in? Do you have friends in Bristol where you could stay?'

Mrs Owen shook her head.

'Then I'll phone the Infirmary and ask them to fix you up—they have a room where you can be comfortable and they'll see that you get a meal. There is a morning bus from Bristol, isn't there? And another one in the late afternoon. I should take an overnight bag.' She added in a gentle matter-of-fact voice, 'Are you all right for ready money, Mrs Owen?'

'Yes thank you, Sister. You don't know how long I might have to stay?'

'Well, no, but I'm sure the ward sister will tell you and you can ask to see Dr Beecham and Dr van Rijgen.'

Mrs Owen went away presently and Fran went into the ward to cast an eye on things and to reassure Mr Owen that his wife would be with him when he was transferred. Other than that there wasn't a great deal to do; she sent the nurses to their dinner and Jenny with them and, leaving the aides in the ward, filling water jugs, went back to her office, where she sat down at her desk and started on the laundry list. She felt restless; perhaps it was the sight of the quiet country she could see from her window, or perhaps it was the knowledge that, after her busy days at the Infirmary, she wasn't working here up to her full capacity. Anyway, she felt unsettled and a little impatient with her life. Was she to go on for ever, living and working in this little country town? Her aunts were dears but they still treated her as though she were a child and she would be twenty-six on her next birthday. Another five years and she would be thirty... She shook her head at her own gloom; nothing ever happened. She turned back to the laundry list and Willy, the porter, came in with the second post. A handful of letters for the patients and one for herself. She got up and went into the wards and handed them all out. Jenny had done the dinners while she had been busy with Mrs Owen and the patients were resting on their beds for an hour. She made her quiet way round the two wards, stopping here and there to have a whispered word, and then went back to the office.

The letter on her desk had a Dutch stamp. It would be from a cousin she hardly knew; the aunts had had a brother who had died and his daughter had married a Dutchman and lived in Holland. Fran remembered her vaguely as a child when her own mother had taken her to visit the family. She had gone to her wedding, too, but although they liked each other their paths didn't cross very frequently.

She opened it now—it would make a nice change from the laundry—and began to read. When she had finished it, she went back to the beginning and read it again. Here was the answer to her restlessness. And one the aunts could not but agree to. Clare wanted her to go and stay. 'You must have some holidays,' she had written, 'two weeks at least. I'm going to have a baby—I was beginning to think that I never would—and I'm so thrilled, I must have someone to talk to about it. I know the aunts make a fuss if you go off on your own, but they can't possibly mind if you stay with us. Do say you'll come—phone me and give me a date. Karel sends his love and says you must come.'

Fran put the letter down. She had two weeks leave

due to her and the wards were slack enough to take them; moreover it was a good time of year to ask before autumn brought its quota of bronchitis and asthma and nasty chests. A holiday might also dispel this feeling of restlessness.

She went to the office after her dinner and asked for leave and Miss Hawkins, aware of Fran's worth, graciously allowed it: starting on the following Sunday, and Sister Manning might add her weekly days off to her fortnight.

All very easy. There were the aunts to deal with, though. Fran, off duty that evening, tackled that the moment she got home. The ladies were sitting, as they always did of an evening, in the old-fashioned drawing room, knitting or embroidering, waiting for Winnie, the housekeeper, to set supper on the table. Fran, poking her head round the door to wish them a good evening before going up to her room to tidy herself, wondered anew at the three of them. They were after all not very old—Aunt Kate was the eldest, sixty-seven, Aunt Polly next, a year or two younger, and Aunt Janet a mere fifty-eight. And yet they had no place in modern times; they lived now as they remembered how they had lived in their childhood years between the two wars. It was only Fran's mother, five years younger than Aunt Janet, who had broken away and married, and had died with Fran's father in a plane crash when Fran had been twelve. She had missed them sorely and her aunts had given her a home and loved her according to their lights, only their love was tempered with selfishness and a determination to keep her with them at all costs. She remembered the various occasions when she had expressed a wish to holiday abroad; they had never raised any objections but one or other of them had fallen ill with something they had referred to as nerves, and each time she had given up her travels and stayed at home to keep the invalid company, fetch and carry and generally pander to that lady's whims. She had been aware that she was being conned, but her kind heart and her sense of obligation wouldn't allow her to say so.

She greeted them now, and whisked herself away and presently went downstairs armed with Clare's letter. Her aunts read it in turn and agreed that, of course, she must go. Looking after a cousin wasn't the same as gallivanting around foreign parts and, as none of them had ever lost their old-fashioned ideas about childbirth—a conglomeration of baby clothes, feeling faint, putting one's feet up and not mentioning the subject because it wasn't quite nice, eating for two and needing the companionship of another woman— they saw that Fran's duty lay in joining her cousin at once. She was, after all, their dear brother's daughter and Fran, they felt sure, was aware where her duty lay.

Fran agreed, careful not to be too eager, and in answer to Aunt Janet's question said that she thought that Matron would allow her to have two weeks, starting on the following Sunday. 'I'd better phone Clare, hadn't I?' she suggested and went to do that, to come back presently to say that Karel would meet her on Sunday evening at Schiphol.

'Sunday?' asked Aunt Kate sharply.

'Well, dear, he's free then, otherwise I'd have to find my own way...'

The conversation at supper was wholly given up to her journey. She said very little, allowing the aunts to discuss and plan and tell her what clothes to take; she had no intention of taking any of their advice but to disagree would be of no use. She helped Winnie clear the supper things presently, laid her breakfast tray ready on the kitchen table, wished her aunts good night and went up to bed. It was too soon to pack, but she went through her wardrobe carefully, deciding what she would take with her. Clare was only a few years older than she was and, contrary to her aunts' supposition, the last person on earth to lie with her feet up; a few pretty dresses would be essential.

There was no time to think about her holiday the next day. Getting Mr Owen away to Bristol was a careful undertaking and necessitated sending Jenny with him. Mrs Owen had arrived, breathless with anxiety and haste, and had had to be given tea and a gentle talk, so that the morning's routine started a good hour late, and that without Jenny to share the chores. Then, of course, there was a new patient coming into Mr Owen's bed and Miss Prosser was making difficulties, something she always did when they were busier than usual. It wasn't until Fran got home at last that she allowed her thoughts to dwell on the delights ahead. She was listening to Aunt Janet's advice about her journey and thinking her own thoughts when the image of Dr van Rijgen popped into her head, and with it a vague but surprising thought that she might not see him again for a long time. Not that I want to, she admonished herself hastily, horrid man that he is, with his nasty sarcastic tongue, and then thought, I wonder where he lives?

Surprisingly he came again at the end of the week, on his way back to Holland, to examine with Dr Beecham one of her patients who, recently returned from the tropics, was showing the first likely symptoms of kala-azar, or so Dr Stokes thought. To be on the safe side, Fran had put her in the single ward and had nursed her in strict isolation, so that they were all gowned and masked before they went to see the patient. Dr van Rijgen, being tied into a gown a good deal too small for his vast person, stared at Fran over his mask. 'Let us hope your praiseworthy precautions will prove unnecessary, Sister,' he said. She caught the faint sneer in his voice and blushed behind her own mask. She had, after all, only done what Dr Stokes had ordered; he had spoken as though she had panicked into doing something unnecessary.

Which, after a lengthy examination, proved to be just that. Acute malarial infection, pronounced Dr van Rijgen. 'Which I think can be dealt with quite satisfactorily here. It is merely a question of taking a blood sample to discover which drug is the most suitable. I think we might safely give a dose of chloroquinine phosphate and sulphate…' He held out a hand for the chart Fran was holding and began to write, talking to Dr Stokes at the same time. 'You were right to take precautions, Peter, one can never be too careful.' A remark which Fran considered to be just the kind of thing he would delight in; buttering up Dr Stokes after sneering at her for doing exactly the same thing.

He had the effrontery to look at her and smile, too, as he said it. She gave him a story stare and led the way to the office where she dispensed coffee to the three of them and ignored him. It was as they were about to leave that Dr van Rijgen asked, 'Who takes over from you when you go on holiday, Sister?'

'My staff nurse, Jenny Topps.'

'I believe you start your leave on Sunday?'

'Yes,' and, after a pause, 'sir'.

He looked at her from under his lids. 'A pleasant time to go on holiday. Somewhere nice I hope?'

'Yes.'

It was vexing when Dr Beecham chimed in with, 'Well, the girl can't say anything else, can she, seeing that she is going to your country, Litrik?'

'Indeed! Let us hope the weather remains fine for you, Sister. Good morning.'

When they had gone she sat and fumed at her desk for a few minutes. He had been nastier than usual and she hoped that she would never see him again. She got up and when she'd done her desk went in search of Jenny; it was almost time for the patients' dinners and the two diabetic ladies would need their insulin. There were several patients whom Dr Beecham wanted put on four-hourly charts, too. She became absorbed in the ward's routine and, for the time at least, forgot Dr van Rijgen.

There was a day left before she was to go on holiday; it was fully taken up with handing over to Jenny and, when she went off duty that evening, packing.

Her head stuffed with sound advice from her aunts, just as though she were on her way to darkest Africa, she took the early morning bus to Bristol where she caught a train to London, got on the underground to Heathrow and presented herself at the weighing-in counter with half an hour to spare. There was time for a cup of coffee before her flight was called and she sat drinking it and looking around her. A small, neat girl, wearing a short-sleeved cotton dress, sparkling fresh, high-heeled sandals, and carrying a sensible shoulder bag. She attracted quite a few appreciative glances from passers-by, together with their opinion that she was the kind of traveller who arrived looking as band-box fresh as when she had set out.

They were right; she arrived at Schiphol without a hair out of place, to be met by Karel and driven to Bloemendaal, a charming suburb of Haarlem where he and Clare had a flat. It wasn't a lengthy trip but they had plenty to talk about: the baby, of course, his job—he was an accountant in one of the big bulb growers' offices—Clare's cleverness in learning Dutch, the pleasant life they led…

The flat was in a leafy road, quiet and pleasant, within walking distance of the dunes and woods. They lived on the third floor and Clare was waiting at their door as the lift stopped. She was a pretty girl, a little older than Fran, and she flung her arms round her now, delighted to see her. The pair of them led her into the flat, both talking at once, sitting her down between them in the comfortable living room, plying her with questions. After the aunts' staid and sober conversation, they were a delight to Fran.

Presently Clare bore her off to her room where she unpacked and tidied herself and then joined them for tea and a lively discussion as to how she might best enjoy herself.

'Swimming of course,' declared Clare, 'if the weather holds.' She poured more tea. 'I rest in the afternoons, so you can poke around Haarlem if you want to. There is heaps to see if you like churches and museums. Then there is Linnaeushof Gardens and the open air theatre here and the aviary... Two weeks won't be enough.'

'You are dears to have me,' said Fran. 'It's lovely to—to...'

'Escape?' suggested Clare.

Fran, feeling guilty, said yes.

It was a delightful change after life in the hospital; Karel went early to work and she and Clare breakfasted at their leisure, tidied the flat and then took a bus into Haarlem or did a little shopping at the local shops; and after lunch, Clare curled up with a book and Fran took herself off, walking in the dunes, going into Haarlem, exploring its streets, poking her nose into its many churches, visiting its museums, and window shopping.

It was on the fourth day of her visit when she went back to St Bavo's Cathedral. She had already paid it a brief visit with Clare on one of their morning outings but Clare hadn't much use for old churches. It was a brilliant afternoon so that the vast interior seemed bathed in twilight and she pottered happily, straining to see the model ships hanging from its lofty rafters, trying to understand the ornate memorial stones on its walls and finally standing before the organ, a vast affair with its three keyboards and its five thousand pipes. Her mind boggled at anyone attempting to play it and, as if in answer to that, music suddenly flooded from it so that she sat down to listen, enthralled. It was something grand and stirring and yet sad and solemn; she had heard it before but the composer eluded her. She closed her eyes the better to hear and became aware that someone had come to sit beside her.

'Fauré,' said Dr van Rijgen. 'Magnificent, isn't it? He is practising for the International Organists' Contest.'

Fran's eyes had flown open. 'However did you get here?' And then, absurdly, 'Good afternoon, Dr van Rijgen. I was trying to remember the composer—the organist is playing like a man inspired.'

She studied his face for a moment; somehow he seemed quite friendly. 'Do you live here?'

'Utrecht.'

'But that's the other side of Amsterdam…'

'Thirty-eight miles from here. Less than that; I don't need to go to Amsterdam, there is a road south…'

She was aware that the music had become quiet and sad. 'You have patients here?'

'What a girl you are for asking questions. I came to see if you were enjoying your holiday.'

She goggled at him. 'Whatever for? And how did you know where I was staying, anyway?'

He smiled slowly. 'Oh, ways and means. Your cousin told me you would most probably be here. She most kindly invited me back for tea. I'll drive you, but there's time enough. Shall we wait till the end? The best part, I always think.'

Fran opened her mouth and then closed it again. What was there to say in the face of such arrogance, short of telling him to go away, not easily done in church, somehow? But why had he deliberately come looking for her? She sat and pondered the question while the organ thundered and swelled into a crescendo of sound and faded away to a kind of sad triumph.

Dr van Rijgen stirred. 'Magnificent. Do you like our *Grote Kirk?*'

'It's breathtaking; I didn't know it was so old…all those years building it. I must get a book about it.'

'I have several at home; you must borrow one.'

Fran stood up and he stood up with her, which put her at an instant disadvantage for she had to look up to his face. 'You want something, don't you?' she asked. 'I mean,' she hesitated and blushed. 'You don't—you aren't interested in me as—as a person, are you?'

'That, Francesca, is where you are mistaken. I should add that I have not fallen in love with you or any such foolishness, but as a person, yes, I am interested in you.'

'Why?'

She spoke softly because there were people milling all round them now.

'At the proper time I will tell you. Now, if you are ready, shall we go back to your cousin?'

She went ahead of him, down the length of the vast church, her mind in a fine muddle. But I don't even like him, she reminded herself, and then frowned quite fiercely. Once or twice during their strange talk, she had liked him very much.

CHAPTER TWO

SHE paused outside the great entrance to the church and he touched her arm. 'Over here, Francesca,' he said and led her to a silver grey Daimler parked at the side. On the short drive to Clare's flat he made casual conversation which gave Fran no chance to ask questions and once there she saw that she was going to have even less opportunity. Apparently whatever it was he wanted of her would be made clear in his own good time and not before. And since she had no intention of seeing him again while she was in Holland, he would presently get the surprise he deserved.

Her satisfaction was short-lived. She was astounded to hear him calmly telling Clare that he felt sure that she would like to see something of Holland while she was there, and would Clare mind if he came on the following day and took her guest for a run through the more rural parts of the country?

She was still struggling for words when she heard Clare's enthusiastic, 'What a marvellous idea! She'll love it, won't she, Karel?'

Just as though I'm not here, fumed Fran silently, and got as far as, 'But I don't...'

'Oh, don't mind leaving Clare for a day,' said Karel. 'I shall be taking her to the clinic tomorrow anyway—you go off and have fun.' He gave her a kindly smile and Fran almost choked on the idea of having fun with Dr van Rijgen. Whatever it was he wanted of her would have nothing to do with fun. She amended the thought; perhaps not fun, but interesting? All the same, such high-handed behaviour wouldn't do at all. She waited until there was a pause in the conversation. 'I had planned to visit one or two places,' she said clearly and was stopped by Dr van Rijgen.

'Perhaps another day for those?' he suggested pleasantly. 'It would give me great pleasure to show you some small part of my country, Francesca.'

There was nothing to say in the face of that bland politeness. She agreed to go, the good manners the aunts had instilled into her from an early age standing her in good stead.

He left shortly after with the suggestion that he might call for her soon after nine o'clock the next morning.

'Don't you like him?' asked Clare the moment the sound of his car had died away.

'Well,' observed Fran matter-of-factly, 'I don't really know him, do I? He gave us lectures when I was training and he's given me instructions about patients on the wards... He was absolutely beastly to me when I was a student and I dozed off during one of his lectures. I think he laughs at me.'

Clare shot her a quick look, exchanged a lightning glance with Karel and said comfortably, 'Oh, well, I should think he's forgotten about that by now—or perhaps he is making amends.'

A fair girl, Fran said, 'I shouldn't have fallen asleep, you know—I expect it injured his ego.'

Clare gave a little chortle of laughter. 'You know, love, once you've got to know each other, I think you and Dr van Rijgen might have quite a lot in common. He's very well known over here; did you know that?'

'No. He comes to Bristol to lecture on tropical diseases, that's all I know about him.'

'Well, he goes to London and Edinburgh and Birmingham and Vienna and Brussels—you name it and he has been there. A very clever laddie.'

Fran had turned her head to look out of the window; Fran was a dear and Clare studied her... She was a thought old-fashioned but that was the aunts' fault, and save for her lovely eyes she had no looks to speak of. But, her hair was fine and long, and her figure was good, if a trifle plump. Clare, with all the enthusiasm of the newly wed, scented romance.

There was no romance apparent the following morning. Dr van Rijgen arrived exactly when he said he would, spent five minutes or so charming Clare—there was no other word for it, thought Fran indignantly—and then led the way to his car.

'Where are we going?' asked Fran and, when he didn't answer at once, 'where are you taking me?'

He was driving south, through the country roads criss-crossing the *duinen* so that he might avoid Haarlem, and there was very little traffic about. He pulled

in to the side of the road and turned to look at her.
'Shall we clear the air, Francesca? You sound like the
heroine in a romantic thriller. I'm not taking you anywhere, not in the sense that you imply. We shall drive
across country, avoiding the motorways so that you
may be able to see some of the more rural parts of
Holland, and then we shall go to my home because I
should like you to meet someone there.'

'Your wife,' said Fran instantly.

'My wife is dead.' He started up the car once more.
'On our right you can just get a glimpse of Heem-
stede, a suburb of Haarlem and very pleasant. And
down the road is Vogelenzang, a quite charming
stretch of wooded dunes; we must go there one day
to hear the birds...'

Fran turned her head away and pretended to take
an interest in the scenery; she had been snubbed, there
were no two ways about that. If these terms were to
continue all day then she began to wish most heartily
that she had never come; she hadn't wanted to in the
first place. She voiced her thoughts out loud.

'No, that was only too obvious, but it was rather
difficult for you to refuse, wasn't it?'

'I cannot think,' said Fran crossly, 'why you are
bothering to waste your time with me.'

'I dare say not, but now is not the time to explain.
And now, if you could forget your dislike of me for
an hour or two, I will tell you where we are going.
This road takes us the long way round to Aalsmeer.
We shall go through Hillegom very shortly and take

a secondary road to the shores of Aalsmeer which will take us to the town itself; there we shall drive down its other shore and take country roads, some of them narrow and brick, to Nieuwkoop. We have to drive right round the northern end of the lake and pick up the road which eventually brings us to the motorway into Utrecht. My home is on the far side of the city in the woods outside Zeist. We will stop for coffee at one of the cafés along the Aalsmeer.'

'It sounds a long way,' observed Fran.

'No distance as the crow flies, and not much further by car. We shall lunch at my home.'

She gave him a sideways glance. His profile looked stern; he couldn't possibly be enjoying himself so why had he asked her out? He turned his head before she could look away. His smile took years off his face. 'I haven't had a day out for a long time—shall we forget hospital wards and night duty and lectures by disagreeable doctors and enjoy ourselves?'

His smile was so warm and friendly that she smiled back. 'Oh, I'd like that—and it's such a lovely day.'

His hand came down briefly on hers clasped in her lap. 'It's a pact. Here we are at Aalsmeer. I'll explain about the flowers...'

They stopped for coffee presently, sitting down by the water's edge while he drew a map of the surrounding countryside on the tablecloth. 'There are motorways coming into Utrecht from each point of the compass. We shall join one to the south, going

round the city, and then turn off towards Leusder-
heide—that's heathland…'

'You live there?'

'No, but very near. It's only a short run from here.'

They got back into the car and drove on through
the quiet countryside with only the farms and small
villages studded around the flat green fields. But not
for long. They joined the motorway very soon and
presently the outskirts of Utrecht loomed ahead and
then to one side of them as they swept past the outskirts. Dr van Rijgen drove fast with an ease which
was almost nonchalance, slipping past the traffic with
nothing more than a gentle swish of sound, and once
past Utrecht and with Zeist receding in the distance
he left the motorway and slowed his speed. They were
on a country road now, with Zeist still visible to one
side, and on the other pleasantly wooded country,
peaceful after the rush of the motorway.

'We could be miles from anywhere,' marvelled
Fran.

'Yes, and I need only drive a couple of miles to
join the road into Zeist and Utrecht.'

'And the other way?'

'Ede, Appeldoorn, the Veluwe; all beautiful.'

'You go there often, to the—the Veluwe?'

He didn't allow himself to smile at her pronunci-
ation of the word.

'Most weekends when I am free.'

It was like wringing blood from a stone, she reflected, wringing bits and pieces of information from

him, word by word. She gave a small soundless sigh and looked out of the window.

They were passing through a small scattered village: tiny cottages, a very large church and a number of charming villas.

'This looks nice,' she observed.

'I think so, too,' said Dr van Rijgen and swept the car with an unexpected rush through brick pillars and along a leafy drive. Fran, suddenly uneasy, sat up, the better to see around her, just in time to glimpse the house as they went round a curve.

It was flat-faced and solid with a gabled roof and large windows arranged in rows across its front; they got smaller and higher as they went up and they all had shutters. The front door was atop semi-circular steps, a solid wooden affair with ornate carving around its fanlight and a tremendous knocker.

Fran didn't look at the doctor. 'You live here?'

'Yes.' He leaned over her and undid her door and her safety belt and then got out himself and went round the bonnet so that he was standing waiting for her as she got out, too. She said quite sharply, 'I wish you would tell me why you've brought me here.'

'Why, to meet my small daughter. She's looking forward to seeing you.'

'Your daughter? I had no idea…'

He said coolly, 'Why should you have? Shall we go in?'

The door had been opened; a very thin, stooping, elderly man was standing by it. 'Tuggs,' said the doctor, 'this is Miss Manning, come to have lunch with us. Francesca, Tuggs has been with us for very many years; he runs the place with his wife, Nel. He is English, by the way.'

Fran paused at the top of the steps and offered a hand. 'How do you do, Tuggs,' and smiled her gentle smile before she was ushered indoors.

It was a square entrance hall with splendid pillars supporting a gallery above it and with a fine staircase at its end. Fran had the impression of marble underfoot, fine silky carpets, a great many portraits, and sunlight streaming through a circular window above the staircase, before she was urged to enter a room at the back of the hall. She paused in the doorway and looked up at her host. 'I'm a bit overwhelmed—it's so very grand.'

He considered this remark quite seriously. 'One's own home is never grand, and it is home. Don't be scared of it, Francesca.' He shut the door behind them. 'Nel will bring coffee in a few moments and you can go and tidy yourself—she'll show you where. But first come and see Lisa.'

They were in a quite small cosy room with chintz curtains at the windows and a wide view out to a garden filled with flowers. The furniture was old, polished and comfortable, and sitting by the open window was a buxom young woman with a rosy face, reading to a little girl perched in a wheelchair.

The young woman, looking up, saw them, put down her book and said something to the child who turned her head and shrilled, 'Papa!' and then burst into a torrent of Dutch.

She was a beautiful child, with golden curls, enormous blue eyes and a glorious smile. Dr van Rijgen bent to kiss her and then lifted her carefully into his arms. He said something to the nurse and she smiled and went out of the room and he said,

'This is Lisa, six years old and as I frequently tell her the most beautiful girl in the world.'

Fran took a small thin hand in hers. 'Oh, she is, the darling.' She beamed at the little girl, careful not to look at the fragile little body in the doctor's arms. 'Hullo, Lisa.'

The child put up her face to be kissed and broke into a long excited speech until the doctor hushed her gently. 'Let's sit down for a moment,' he suggested and glanced up as a stout woman came in with a tray. 'Here's Nel with the coffee.' He said something to her and turned to Fran.

'This is my housekeeper; no English worth mentioning, I'm afraid, but a most sensible and kind woman; we'd be lost without her.' He spoke to her again—she was being introduced in her turn, Fran guessed—and then got up as he said, 'Nel will show you where you can tidy yourself.'

The cloakroom into which Fran was ushered, tucked away down a short passage leading from the hall, was so unlike the utilitarian cubby hole in her aunts' house that she paused to take a good look. Powder blue tiles, silver grey carpet, an enormous mirror and a shelf containing just about everything a woman might need to repair the ravages upon her make-up. Fran sniffed appreciatively at the bottles of eau-de-toilette, washed her hands with pale blue soap and felt apologetic about using one of the stack of towels. She dabbed powder on her nose in a perfunctory manner, combed her hair and went back across the hall.

Father and daughter looked at her as she went in and she had the strong impression that they had been talking about her—naturally enough, she supposed; and when asked to pour out she did so in her usual unflurried manner.

Lisa had milk in her own special mug and sugar biscuits on a matching plate but they were largely ignored. She was a happy child, chuckling a great deal at her father's soft remarks, meticulously translated for Fran's benefit.

A very sick child, too, the charming little face far too pale, the small body thin above the sticks of useless legs. But there was no hint of despair or sadness; the doctor drew her into the talk, making a great thing of translating for her and urging her to try out a few Dutch words for herself, something which sent Lisa into paroxysms of mirth. Presently she demanded to sit on Fran's lap, where she sat, Fran's firm arm holding her gently, examining her face and hair, chattering non-stop.

They were giggling comfortably together when the young woman came back and Dr van Rijgen said,

'This is Nanny. She has been with us for almost six years and is quite irreplaceable. She speaks little English. Lisa goes for a short rest now before lunch.'

Fran said, 'How do you do, Nanny,' feeling doubtful that such an old and tried member of the family might look upon her with jealousy. It was a relief to see nothing but friendliness in the other girl's face and, what was more puzzling, a kind of excited expectancy.

Alone with her host, Fran sat back and asked composedly, 'Will you tell me about Lisa? It's not spina bifida—she's paralysed isn't she, the poor darling? Is it a meningocele?'

He sounded as though he was delivering a lecture on the ward. 'Worse than that—a myelomeningocele, paralysis, club feet and a slight hydrocephalus.' His voice was expressionless as he added, 'Everything that could be done, has been done; she has at the most six more months.'

The words sounded cold; she studied his face and saw what an effort it was for him to speak calmly. She said quietly, 'She is such a happy child and you love her. She would be easy to love…'

'I would do anything in the world to keep her happy.' He got up and walked over to the french window at the end of the room and opened it and two dogs came in: a mastiff and a roly-poly of a dog, very low on the ground with a long curly coat and bushy eyebrows almost hiding liquid brown eyes.

'Meet Thor and Muff—Thor's very mild unless

he's been put on guard, but Muff seems to think that he must protect everyone living here.'

He wasn't going to say any more about Lisa. Fran asked, 'Why Muff?'

'He looks like one, don't you think?' He bent to tweak the dog's ears. 'Would you like to see the gardens? Lisa spends a good deal of time out here when the weather's fine.'

There was a wide lawn beyond the house bordered by flower beds and trees. They wandered on for a few minutes in silence, with the doctor, the perfect host, pointing out this and that and the other thing which might interest her. But presently he began to ask her casual questions about her work, her home and her plans.

'I haven't any,' said Fran cheerfully. 'I would have liked to have stayed on at the Infirmary; at least I'd have had the chance to carve myself a career, but the aunts needed me at home.'

'They are invalids?'

'Heavens no, nothing like that. They—they just feel that—that…'

'You should be at their beck and call,' he finished for her smoothly.

'Oh, you mustn't say that. They gave me a home and I'm very grateful.'

'To the extent of turning your back on your own future? Have you no plans to marry?'

'None at all,' she told him steadily.

He didn't ask any more questions after that, but

turned back towards the house, offering a glass of sherry while they waited for Lisa to join them for lunch.

She sat between them, eating with the appetite of a bird, talking non-stop, and Fran, because it amused the child, tried out a few Dutch words again. Presently they went into the garden once more, pushing the wheelchair, Fran naming everything in sight in English at Lisa's insistence.

They had tea under an old mulberry tree in the corner of the garden and when Nanny came to take her away, Lisa demanded with a charm not to be gainsaid, 'Fran is to come again, Papa—tomorrow?'

He was lying propped up against the tree, watching her. 'Are you doing anything tomorrow?' he asked. 'We might take Lisa to the sea—the sand's firm enough for the chair.'

'If she would like me to come, then I will—I'd like to very much.'

She was quite unprepared for the joy on the child's face as her father told her. Two thin arms were wrapped round her neck and she was kissed heartily. In between kisses she said something to her father and squealed with delight at his reply. Fran looked from one to the other of them, sensing a secret, probably about herself. She certainly wasn't going to ask, she told herself, and wished Nanny goodbye, encountering that same look of pleased anticipation. It was time she went home, she decided and was instantly and blandly talked out of it.

They dined in a leisurely fashion in a room furnished with an elegant Regency-style oval table and ribbon-backed chairs and a vast side table laden with heavy silver. Fran was surprised to find her companion easy to talk to and the conversation was light and touched only upon general topics. Lisa wasn't mentioned and although she longed to ask more about the child, she was given no opportunity to pose any questions.

She was driven back to Clare's flat, her companion maintaining a pleasant flow of small talk which gave away nothing of himself. And at the flat, although he accepted her invitation to go in with her, he stayed only a short time before bidding them all good night and reiterating that he would call for her at ten o'clock in the morning.

Clare pounced on her the moment he had gone. 'Fran—you dark horse—did you know he'd be here? Did he follow you over to Holland?'

Fran started to collect the coffee cups. 'Nothing like that, love, we don't even like each other. He has a small daughter who is very ill; I think he has decided that it might amuse her to have a visitor. We got on rather well together, so I suppose that's why he's asked me to go out with them tomorrow.'

'His wife?' breathed Clare, all agog.

'He is a widower.'

'And you don't like each other?'

'Not really. He's devoted to Lisa, though, and she

liked me. I like her, too. You won't mind if I'm away tomorrow?'

Her cousin grinned. 'You have fun while you've got the chance.'

The weather was being kind; Fran awakened to a blue sky and warm sunshine. She was ready and waiting when Dr van Rijgen and Lisa arrived. She got in beside Lisa's specially padded seat in the back of the car and listened, only half understanding, to the child's happy chatter.

It was a successful day, she had to admit to herself as she got ready for bed that evening. They had gone to Noordwijk-aan-zee, parked the car and carried Lisa and her folded chair down to the water's edge where the sand was smooth and firm. They had walked miles, with the shore stretching ahead of them for more miles, and then stopped off for crusty rolls and hard-boiled eggs. They had talked and laughed a lot and little Lisa had been happy, her pale face quite rosy; and as for the doctor, Fran found herself almost liking him. It was a pity, she reflected, jumping into bed, that he would be at the hospital at Utrecht for all of the following day; it was even more of a pity that he hadn't so much as hinted at seeing her again. 'Not that I care in the least,' she told herself. 'When Lisa isn't there he is a very unpleasant man.' Upon which somewhat arbitrary thought she went to sleep.

She spent the next morning quietly with Clare and Karel, and took herself for a walk in the afternoon. Another week, and her holiday would be over. She hadn't mentioned Dr van Rijgen in her letters to the aunts and upon reflection she decided not to say anything about him. She thought a great deal about little Lisa, too; a darling child and happy; she had quite believed the doctor when he had said that he would do anything to keep her so. She went back to the flat, volunteered to cook the supper while Clare worried away at some knitting and went to bed early, declaring that she was tired.

Karel had gone to work and she was giving Clare the treat of breakfast in bed when the doctor telephoned. He would be at the hospital all the morning, he informed her in a cool voice, but he hoped that she would be kind enough to spend the afternoon with Lisa. 'I'll call for you about half past one,' he told her and rang off before she could say a word.

'Such arrogance,' said Fran crossly. 'Anyone would think I was here just for his convenience.'

All the same, she was ready, composed and a little cool in her manner when he arrived. A waste of effort on her part for he didn't seem to notice her stand-offish manner. To her polite enquiries as to his morning, he had little to say, but launched into casual questions. When was she returning home? What did she think of Holland? Did she find the language difficult to understand? And then, harshly, did she feel at her ease with Lisa?

Fran turned to look at him in astonishment. 'At ease? Why ever shouldn't I? She's a darling child and the greatest fun to be with. I like children.' She sounded so indignant that he said instantly, 'I'm sorry, I put that badly.' He turned the car into the drive. 'A picnic tea, don't you think? It's such a lovely day.' And, as she got out of the car, 'It would be nice, if you are free tomorrow, if you will come with us to the Veluwe—it's charming, rather like your New Forest, and Lisa sees fairies behind every tree. We'll fetch you about half past ten?'

'I haven't said I'll come,' observed Fran frostily, half in and half out of the car.

'Lisa wants you.'

And that's the kind of left-handed compliment a girl likes having, thought Fran, marching ahead of him up the steps, her ordinary nose in the air.

But she forgot all that when Lisa joined them; in no time at all, she was laughing as happily as the little girl, struggling with the Dutch Lisa insisted upon her trying out. They had tea on the lawn again and when Nanny came to fetch Lisa to bed, Fran went, too, invited by both Nanny and the child.

Being got ready for bed was a protracted business dealt with by Nanny with enviable competence. But it was fun, too. Fran fetched and carried and had a satisfactory conversation with Nanny even though they both spoke their own language for the most part. They sat on each side of Lisa while she ate her supper and then at last was carried to her small bed in the charming nursery. Here Fran kissed her good night and went back to the day nursery, because it was Nanny's right to tuck her little charge up in bed and give her a final hug. She had just joined Fran when the doctor came in, said something to Nanny and went through to the night nursery where there was presently a good deal of giggling and murmuring before he came back.

He talked to Nanny briefly, wished her good night and swept Fran downstairs.

They had drinks by the open windows in the drawing-room and presently dined. Fran, who was hungry, ate with a good appetite, thinking how splendid it must be to have a super cook to serve such food and someone like Tuggs to appear at your elbow whenever you wanted something. They didn't talk much, but their silences were restful; the doctor wasn't a man you needed to chat to, thank heaven.

They had their coffee outside in the still warm garden, with the sky darkening and the faint scent of the roses which crowded around the lawn mingling with the coffee. She sighed and the doctor asked, 'What are you thinking, Francesca?'

'That it's very romantic and what a pity it's quite wasted on us.'

She couldn't see his face, but his voice was casual. 'We are perhaps beyond the age of romance.'

She snapped back before she could stop herself, 'I'm twenty-five!'

'On October the third you will be twenty-six. I shall be thirty-seven in December.'

'However did you know?' began Fran.

'I made it my business to find out.' His voice was

so mild that she choked back several tart remarks fighting for utterance.

'More coffee?' she asked finally.

Their day in the Veluwe was a success: the doctor might be a tiresome man but he was a splendid father and, when he chose to be, a good host. They drove through the narrow lanes criss-crossing the Veluwe and picnicked in a charming clearing with the sunshine filtering through the trees and numerous birds. The food was delicious: tiny sausage rolls, bite-size sandwiches, chicken vol-au-vents, hard-boiled eggs, crisp rolls and orange squash to wash them down. Fran, watching Lisa, saw that she ate very little and presently, tucked in her chair, she fell asleep.

When she woke up, they drove on, circling round to avoid the main roads and getting back in time for a rather late tea. This time the doctor was called away to the telephone and returned to say that he would have to go to Utrecht that evening. Fran said at once, 'Then if you'll give me a lift to the city I'll get a bus.'

'Certainly not.' He sat down beside Lisa and explained at some length and then said, 'Lisa quite understands—this often happens. We'll get Nanny and say good night and leave at once; there will be plenty of time to drive you to your cousin's flat.'

And nothing she could say would alter his plans.

It was two days before she saw him again. Pleasant enough, pottering around with Clare, going out for a quiet drive in the evenings when Karel got home, all the same she felt a tingle of pleasure when the doctor telephoned. She had only two days left and she was beginning to think that she wouldn't see him or Lisa again.

'A farewell tea party,' he explained. 'I'll pick you up on my way back from Zeist—about two o'clock.'

He hung up and her pleasure turned to peevishness. 'Arrogant man!'

All the same she greeted him pleasantly when he arrived, listened to his small talk as they drove towards his home and took care not to mention the fact that in two days time she would be gone. He knew, anyway, she reminded herself; it was to be a farewell tea party.

Lisa was waiting for them, sitting in her chair under the mulberry tree. She wound her arms round Fran's neck, chattering away excitedly. 'Is it a birthday or something?' asked Fran. 'There's such an air of excitement.'

Father and daughter exchanged glances. 'You shall know in good time,' said the doctor blandly.

They took their time over tea, talking in a muddled but satisfactory way with Fran struggling with her handful of Dutch words and the doctor patiently translating for them both. But presently Nanny arrived and Lisa went with her without a word of protest.

'I'll see her to say goodbye?' she asked, turning to wave.

Dr van Rijgen didn't answer that. He said instead, in a perfectly ordinary voice, 'I should like you to marry me, Francesca.'

She sat up with a startled yelp and he said at once, 'No, be good enough to hear me out. May I say at once that it is not for the usual reasons that I wish to marry you; since Lisa was able to talk she has begged me for a mama of her own. Needless to say I began a search for such a person but none of my women friends were suitable. Oh, they were kind and pleasant to Lisa but they shrank from contact with her. Besides, she didn't like any of them. You see, she had formed her own ideas of an ideal mama—someone small and gentle and mouselike, who would laugh with her and never call her a poor little girl. When I saw you at the prize giving at the Infirmary I realised that you were exactly her ideal. I arranged these days together so that you might get to know her—needless to say, you are perfect in her eyes...'

'The nerve, the sheer nerve!' said Fran in a strong voice. 'How can you dare...?'

'I think I told you that I would do anything for Lisa to keep her happy until she dies. I meant it. She has six months at the outside and you have fifty— sixty years ahead of you. Do you grudge a few months of happiness to her? Of course, it will be a marriage in name only and when the time comes,' his voice was suddenly harsh, 'the marriage can be annulled without fuss and you will be free to resume your career. I shall see that it doesn't suffer on our account.'

Fran gazed at him, speechless. She was more than surprised; she was flabbergasted. Presently, since the silence had become lengthy, she said, 'It's ridiculous, and even if I were to consider it, I'd need time to decide.'

'There is nothing ridiculous about it if you ignore your own feelings on the matter, and there is no time. Lisa is waiting for us to go to the nursery.'

'And supposing I refuse?'

He didn't answer that. 'You intend to refuse?' There was no reproach in his calm voice, but she knew that, in six months' time, when Lisa's short life had ended, she would never cease to reproach herself.

'No strings?' she asked.

'None. I give you my word.'

'Very well,' said Fran, 'but I'm doing it for Lisa.'

'I hardly imagined that you would do it for me. Shall we go and tell her?'

Lisa was in her dressing-gown, ready for bed, eating something nourishing from a bowl. The face she turned towards them as they went over to her was so full of eager hope that Fran reflected that even if she had refused she would have changed her mind at the sight of it. She felt her hand taken in a firm, reassuring grasp. 'Well, *lieveling,* here is your mama.'

She was aware of Nanny's delighted face as Lisa flung her arms round her neck and hugged her, talking non-stop.

When she paused for breath the doctor said, 'Lisa wants to know when and where. I think the best thing is for me to drive you back and you can discuss it with your aunts. And for reasons which I have already mentioned the wedding will have to be here.' He smiled a little. 'And you must wear a bride's dress and a veil.'

Fran looked at him over Lisa's small head. 'Anything to make her happy.'

He said gravely, 'At least we can agree upon that.'

CHAPTER THREE

THEY stayed with Lisa for some time; she was excited and happy, talking nineteen to the dozen, full of plans for a future which would never be hers, but presently she became drowsy and the doctor carried her to bed where she fell instantly asleep.

Downstairs in the drawing room, over drinks and with the dogs at their feet, Dr van Rijgen observed, 'Thank you, Francesca, you have made Lisa happy. Now as to plans for the future… For a start, you must call me Litrik and, with Lisa, we must present at the least a friendly front. I suggest that I drive you home and we can tell your aunts together. You realise why the wedding must be here, of course? Lisa expects a full-blown affair, I'm afraid, and you are free to invite anyone you wish to attend. Are your aunts likely to disapprove?'

'Disapprove. Well, I don't know. You see they have made up their minds that I shan't marry, but I think that if we just told them at once they wouldn't be able to do much about it. I don't want them to know the real reason…'

'God forbid. How soon can you be free to marry me? It will take about three weeks for the formalities here.'

'I can be ready by then. It might help if you wrote to Miss Hawkins…'

'I'll go and see her. Do you want Dr Beecham to give you away? The service isn't the same as your Church of England, but I dare say you'll feel better if it's on familiar lines.'

It was rather like discussing the future treatment for a patient and just as impersonal and efficient.

'That would be nice.' She swallowed the rest of her sherry and wished that it would warm her cold insides.

'I will arrange your return here and for any family or friends whom you would like at our wedding.' He got up and refilled her glass.

'I must reassure you that you will be free to return to England after Lisa's death.' His voice was bleak. 'The annulment may take a little time but it can be dealt with here; you will have no need to be bothered with it.'

Fran tossed off her sherry. 'You had it all worked out, didn't you? Were you so sure of me?'

He smiled faintly. 'Certainly not. But Lisa was.' He got up and took her glass as Tuggs came in to say that dinner was served. 'And may I, on behalf of Mrs Tuggs and myself, wish you both happiness, Miss Manning and you, sir.'

'Why thank you, Tuggs. I shall be driving Miss Manning back the day after tomorrow; when I return we must make all the necessary arrangements. We hope to marry within the month.'

Nothing more was said about the wedding over dinner and when Fran said that she would like to go back to Clare's, Litrik made no objection. It was a warm quiet night and they had little to say to each other. Only when he drew up before Clare's flat did Litrik say, 'I'll come in with you, if I may—it may be easier for you.'

Karel and Clare were delighted at the news. Beyond remarking that it must have been love at first sight, and the hope that they would wait until she had had the baby before they married, Clare showed little surprise. She plied them with coffee and then tactfully retired to her kitchen with Karel so that Fran could bid her new fiancé good night—something she did in her normal calm manner, thanking him for her pleasant afternoon and asking if he would be good enough to let her know when he wished her to be ready for the journey back to England.

'Well, I'll let you know tomorrow. You will have to come and say goodbye to Lisa. Can you manage the morning? I've patients to see after lunch.'

'Very well.' She hesitated. 'I think I must be mad,' she said suddenly.

'No—compassionate, kind of heart and trusting, but never mad.' He was at the door. 'Remember that Lisa loves you.' He said quietly and closed the door softly behind him before she could answer that.

There was no chance of going to bed; Clare and Karel came back and spent the next hour talking about the momentous news. 'It's fabulous!' declared

Clare. 'Fran, he's rich, and I mean rich, and well known and you'll have just about everything you can possibly want. I'm so thrilled. Whatever will the aunts say?'

'I think they will be struck speechless. I imagine Litrik will convince them; that's why he is going back with me.' Anxious to keep the talk light she added, 'Of course, you'll both come to the wedding, won't you? It won't be more than a month, so you'll be able to come; the baby's not due for about five months, is it?'

'Can't you wait till after Christmas so that I can wear something smart?'

'You'll look smashing—wear layers of chiffon like the models in *Vogue*.' She escaped to her room at last but she was too tired to think clearly by then. She got into bed and went to sleep at once.

She was fetched in the morning by Litrik whose manner towards her couldn't be faulted. He was a naturally reserved man so no one would have expected him to display his feelings in public; nevertheless he managed to convey a loving regard for Fran which more than satisfied Clare. Not that it satisfied Fran. In the car she said forthrightly, 'Are we going to—to pretend all the time? I don't think I'll be much good at it. Calling you dear, and so on.' She turned her head to look at his inscrutable profile. 'You actually sounded as though you are glad that we are going to be married…'

'But I am glad—for Lisa's sake. Is that not a sufficiently good reason? And I am sure that, if you put in some practice, you'll manage a certain warmth towards me. No need to while we are on our own, of course.'

'You are impossible!' declared Fran crossly.

They spent a happy morning nonetheless. Lisa was full of plans for the wedding: the kind of dress Fran was to wear, the food they would eat at the reception, the picnics they would enjoy for the rest of the summer. The doctor translated patiently and when they had at last said goodbye to the child and were driving back to Bloemendaal, Fran remarked, 'I shall have to learn Dutch...I can understand a word here and there but not enough.'

'I'll arrange lessons for you once the wedding is over. In the meantime I know of someone in Bristol who will start you off. Your aunts won't object to her coming each day while you are with them?'

'I don't suppose so. Do I see you again once you have left England?'

'Unlikely. I will keep you informed as to plans. You do realise that you will need to wear bride's clothes? Lisa expects that.'

'You mean a veil and bouquet and a white dress? Yes, I know.'

'Good. Have you sufficient money, Francesca?'

Even if she hadn't a penny, she wouldn't have admitted it. 'Yes, thank you. At what time do we go tomorrow?'

'I'll be at your cousin's flat about nine o'clock.

We'll go over by hovercraft from Calais. We should be with your aunts by teatime or a little after.'

Clare and Karel saw them off in the morning, her cousin bubbling over with excitement. The two men shook hands like old friends and the doctor made no bones about kissing Clare. 'We shall see you both at the wedding,' were his parting words.

They appeared to be, reflected Fran wryly, the very epitome of blissful love. But once they were on their way, Litrik reverted to his usual slightly mocking calm. 'Lisa sent you a book,' he told her. 'It's in the pocket of your door. You are to look at it and wear a dress exactly like the one she has encircled with chalk.'

It was a picture book telling the story, in a series of most delightful drawings, of a family of mice. And there, on the first page, was Mrs Mouse, in a wide skirted satin dress and a veil crowned with a wreath of orange blossom, her gentle whiskered face peering out from beneath it, tiny paws clasping a Victorian bouquet.

'Oh,' said Fran, and felt a lump in her throat. 'Does she really think of me like that—a mouse…?'

'The highest honour she can bestow on you, Francesca. Please copy the dress as far as possible; I will see that the bouquet is a replica.'

Fran turned the pages; Mrs Mouse's life was busy and happy; there were mouse babies in abundance, suitably bonneted and gowned, and several pictures of the cosy cottage in which they all lived. She said rather gruffly, 'I'll do the best I can about the dress; anything to make her happy.'

His stern profile relaxed. 'Thank you, Francesca.'

It wasn't until they were on the last stage of their journey that they discussed future plans, or rather, the doctor disclosed his plans. She was to leave the hospital within the next few days, merely going there long enough to hand over to Jenny Topps until such time as a new ward sister could be appointed. This, he observed casually, he had already arranged with Miss Hawkins. He would arrange for her to return to Holland in just over three weeks' time, with her aunts or on her own. He had telephoned Dr Beecham who would be delighted to give her away.

'You will, of course stay at my home until the wedding; your aunts, too, of course, and anyone else you may wish to invite.'

He slowed the car as they approached the town, only another five minutes' drive away. 'My own family will be there, of course.'

'Oh.' She was startled out of her usual calm. 'Have you a family?'

He smiled faintly. 'A mother and father, two sisters, nephews and nieces, aunts and uncles. Is that so strange?'

'Yes,' said Fran baldly, 'you don't strike me as being the kind of man to need a family.'

'We have a good deal to learn about each other, Francesca.'

He had stopped before her aunts' house. 'Well, yes,

but it'll be a waste of time, won't it?' A sudden thought struck her. 'Do your family know—I mean why you're marrying me?'

He had got out of the car and had opened her door. 'No, Francesca, no one knows. It will be our secret.'

They walked up the garden path together and at the door he thumped the brass knocker. It was opened almost immediately by Winnie who, after a surprised squawk, cast her arms around Fran. 'Well, love, there's a surprise—tomorrow we thought…' She took a good look at Dr van Rijgen. 'And who's this?'

'Dr van Rijgen, Winnie.' Fran planted a kiss on the elderly cheek. 'We are going to be married, only hush until I've told the aunts.'

Winnie hushed, only pumped the doctor's arm with warmth. 'They are having their tea, like always, in the drawing room.'

Without thinking Fran caught the doctor's hand in hers and led him down the hall and opened the drawing-room door. Her aunts were sitting as they always sat, each in her own particular chair, with Aunt Kate behind the small tea table. She had the teapot in her hand as they went in and when she saw them lowered it carefully on to the tray.

'Francesca—home a day early? You will of course tell us your reason for that. We are pleased to see you home again, child. Polly, ring for more cups and saucers and fresh tea.' Her rather prominent blue eyes were fixed on the doctor, standing by Fran, her hand still on his.

'I don't think we have had the pleasure…' began Aunt Polly.

Fran felt him give her hand a reassuring squeeze. 'Hallo, Aunts,' she said. 'This is Dr van Rijgen— Litrik. We're going to be married and he has driven me back from Holland so that you might meet him.'

The aunts weren't ladies to show their feelings but just for a moment they were caught off balance.

'Married?' asked Aunt Kate, and, 'How romantic,' sighed Aunt Janet, but it was Aunt Polly who rose to the occasion. 'This is unexpected news, you must forgive us if we are surprised. We had no idea…' She left the suggestion of a question in the air, but, since Fran didn't answer it, went on, 'Welcome, Dr van Rijgen, we are delighted to meet you.' She got up and kissed Fran and shook his hand and Aunt Janet and Aunt Kate followed suit before Aunt Kate told them to sit down. 'You will be glad of a cup of tea, of course.' Her eyes had slid to Fran's ringless hand. 'This is very recent, of course. And when do you propose to marry? Next summer, perhaps?'

'In three weeks' time, Miss Askew. In Holland.' Litrik's pleasant voice gave no hint of doubts about that.

'Three weeks—in Holland—that's quite impossible! Francesca, you have your hospital work to consider, and of course, you must be married here.' Aunt Kate, who liked to arrange other people's lives for them, poured their tea with a careless hand, her lips drawn into a thin line.

'Francesca is leaving the hospital in two days' time,' explained Litrik with what Fran secretly decided was his best bedside manner. 'That gives her time to buy anything she wishes for the wedding and join me before the wedding. We both hope that you will all come as our guests and meet my family. And my small daughter. I am a widower.'

He sat back and drank his tea while the three ladies digested this.

'But Holland,' murmured Aunt Polly, making it sound like a remote jungle in some far-flung corner of the globe. 'The church service…'

'Very similar to your own, Miss Askew. I live just outside Utrecht and have a practice there. Francesca will have plenty of friends and her cousin is only a short drive away. And I am well able to support her in comfort.'

'Your daughter…' began Aunt Kate, fighting a losing battle.

'Lisa and Francesca took an instant liking for each other.' He turned to smile at Fran and just for a moment put a hand over hers.

'She's a darling,' said Fran. 'I'm very happy and I hope you will all be happy, too.'

It was Aunt Janet who spoke. 'Of course we are, my dear. We never expected you to marry. We hoped you would be with us always, but it's all very romantic and sudden…'

'Not sudden,' said the doctor surprisingly. 'Francesca and I first met when she was a student nurse at the Infirmary. I go there to give lectures.'

The aunts, who believed in long engagements and knowing each other for years before deciding to get married, looked at him with approval. Here was a man who had taken some years to make up his mind; no flighty youth sweeping their sensible niece off her feet. 'That is different,' pronounced Aunt Kate. 'We should, of course, have preferred to have the wedding here, but you are a man of good sense, I feel sure, and Francesca and we shall be guided by you. You will, of course, stay for the night?'

'Thank you, that is most kind.' He was at his most urbane. 'I should mention that I have to leave by eight o'clock tomorrow morning—I have an appointment for the early evening in Utrecht.'

'All that way,' uttered Aunt Jane. 'You must be tired.'

Fran, casting a quick sideways glance at him, reflected that he wasn't tired at all; that he was enjoying himself in a secret way. Probably he hadn't met anyone like the aunts before.

Winnie was summoned and told to take their guest to his room. 'The car will be quite safe if you drive on to the grass verge by the gate,' he was told. 'Fran, go with Dr van Rijgen and show him.'

It was a lovely evening and the roses smelled sweet. Fran took several happy sniffs and asked, 'Do you mind? Staying the night, I mean?'

'My dear Francesca, I am delighted to do so. When do you report for duty?'

'I wasn't expected until Monday, but I'd like to go in at eight o'clock tomorrow morning.'

He wheeled the car on to the grass verge, got out and locked the doors before he spoke. 'I'll drive you there and have a word with Miss Hawkins.'

'There is no need…'

'Just leave everything to me. I see no possibility of us talking this evening. Do you suppose you could get up earlier and do a little planning over breakfast? Seven o'clock say?'

'The aunts are not called until eight o'clock, but Winnie will be up. I can get our breakfast—we'll have it in the kitchen. It'll be toast and boiled eggs. Winnie does the dining room before she starts cooking.'

They started up the garden path. 'When I'm at home I call the aunts with tea and get my breakfast; that gives Winnie a bit more time…'

'And does no one ever get up and get your breakfast, Francesca?'

'Heavens no!'

They weren't alone again for the rest of the evening; Fran helped Winnie with the supper, unpacked and got her uniform ready for the morning. She also put water, a tin of biscuits and, after an examination of her bookshelf in her room, a copy of an anthology of English verse on his bedside table. The idea of staying up late to talk to Litrik never entered her head.

At least, it entered it, but was discarded at once; with four elderly maiden ladies in the house, it would have thrown a spanner into their stern way of life and quite spoilt the sober picture Litrik had presented.

She was up at half past six the next morning, trotting round the kitchen, laying the table, making tea, cutting bread for toast, boiling eggs. By the time the doctor got down breakfast was ready and they sat down together to eat it, he presenting an impeccable appearance while Fran, mousy hair hanging in soft swathes around her shoulder, buttoned into a sensible dressing-gown Aunt Kate had given her for Christmas, sat unselfconsciously opposite him, gobbling her food as fast as she could. 'I'll not be long dressing,' she told him, 'but I thought I'd better get breakfast over first—I don't suppose you like being kept waiting.'

There was no knowing what he might have replied, for Winnie came in then. Her good morning was severe. 'Miss Fran, you've no business gallivanting around as you are. It's a good thing your aunts can't see you now, sitting there in a dressing-gown—such goings on...'

The doctor's firm mouth twitched although he said nothing. It was Fran who spoke. 'Well, Winnie dear, if you take a good look at the doctor you'll see that he is not the kind of man to tolerate goings on.'

She was biting into her toast as she spoke and didn't look up, which was a pity for the gleam of amusement in the doctor's eye was pronounced. 'Besides,' she added, 'there is nothing of me showing.'

'Miss Fran, I am surprised at you! What the doctor must think!'

He offered his cup for more tea. 'Well, Winnie, times change you know. Francesca and I are to be married very shortly and as she points out, there's nothing visible to upset my normal calm.'

He glanced at his watch. 'Can you be ready in twenty minutes, Francesca?'

Fran bolted the last morsel of toast. 'Yes. Did you say goodbye last night?'

'Yes. I'll be outside in the car.'

She was ready in fifteen minutes, very neat in her uniform, a clean frilled cap perched on to smooth mousy hair. She had been to say good morning to the aunts and goodbye all at the same time, assured them that their guest had slept well and eaten a good breakfast and now she flung an affectionate arm around Winnie's shoulders and nipped down the path to where the car was parked.

'Will it make you late, coming with me?' she asked Litrik.

'No, I have allowed time for that. You have no problems? I will telephone you as soon as I can arrange a date for the wedding—the sooner the better, so try and get your shopping done and the packing within the next ten days or so. Are your aunts likely to delay matters?'

Fran considered. 'Well, they like to do things at

their own pace and arrange things to suit them-selves...'

'Three of the most selfish ladies I have ever met,' declared the doctor blandly. 'If they aren't ready to travel to our wedding then I am afraid they will have to miss it.'

'Well!' observed Fran. 'Well, I never... You mean that.'

'I always mean what I say, Francesca.' He parked the car at the hospital and turned to look at her. 'If they are not ready and willing to travel with you to Holland then I shall expect you on your own.'

She thought of Lisa. 'I'll promise to do that.' She took the picture book for herself from the pocket in the door beside her. 'May I keep this? So that I can copy the dress as nearly as possible. Tell Lisa that, and give her my love.'

They spent fifteen minutes or so with Miss Haw-kins and Fran watched the doctor calmly getting ev-erything all his own way while the unsuspecting Miss Hawkins agreed with all he said. They bade her fare-well presently and Fran went back to the car with him. 'Have a good journey,' she begged him and offered a hand.

He took it and held it fast. 'We shall need to put in some practice,' he observed and bent to kiss her.

She stood watching the car gather speed. She had enjoyed the kiss; perhaps he was beginning to like her and not just because she was marrying him to make Lisa happy. The thought warmed her insides, but only for a moment; when she turned round it was to see faces at most of the windows. He had been seen and had seen them, too, and had acted accordingly; it would have been odd if a newly engaged couple had parted with a hand-shake. The pleasant warmth gave way to rage so her cheeks were fiery with it. The heads at the windows nodded and nudged each other and there were vague remarks about blushing brides, before those of the nursing staff who could leave the wards for a minute or two surged around Fran to offer congratulations.

She received them in her usual calm manner, her cheeks still pink, her eyes sparkling, her thoughts anything but romantic, and presently, since the day's work had to be done, they dispersed to their various duties leaving her and Jenny to go along to her office and begin the job of handing over.

It wasn't just the patients, it was every single article on the wards themselves which had to be accounted for. After a round of the patients and a few instructions to the nurses, the pair of them shut themselves in with a tray of tea and got down to work. Jenny had agreed to take over, at least until the new sister could be appointed, which made things a little easier, for she knew the patients and their treatments and understood the ways of the visiting doctors. All the same, what with the various interruptions from Dr Stokes and the dietitian, the dispensary and the laundry, and, over and above these, the treatments needed by the patients, it was six o'clock before they had finished to their satisfaction. Of course, there was still the ward inventory, a formidable undertaking by Miss Hawkins herself. Fran let Jenny go off duty, made sure that the patients were nicely settled and went into the linen cupboard. She emerged to write the report for the night nurse, phone her aunts to say that she would be home late, and plunged back into the welter of sheets, pillow-cases and blankets. She was still hard at it when the night nurses arrived and it was ten o'clock before she had arranged everything in orderly rows to her satisfaction. In the morning, Jenny could take over the ward, and she would see to the rest. The kitchen wouldn't take long; there was plenty of room in which to lay out crockery and cutlery; the beds could have the bedclothes turned back to make the counting of them easy. The nurses could have time to assemble the contents of the sluice rooms and the bathrooms. Fran went home at last, ate a hasty supper and fell into bed. The aunts would have liked to have talked about the wedding, but there would be time enough for that once she had left the hospital.

The following day was slightly worse although it had its mitigating moments. Fran, gobbling a hasty sandwich after Miss Hawkins's eagle-eyed inspection of ward equipment, was surprised and delighted to find her office suddenly invaded by the other sisters in the hospital, bringing a bottle of sherry with them and a large cardboard box gaily wrapped. She had opened it to find table linen and a rather sentimental card wishing her and Litrik every happiness and she had almost cried at the sight of it. The givers imagined that she was in love and marrying for that reason and she felt sad and guilty all at the same time. And the other good moment of the day was when Dr Beecham came, ruthlessly disturbing Miss Hawkins's inventory, to tell her that he was delighted and more than pleased to be giving her away.

'And I must say you are a fine pair, keeping it dark until the last moment. The wife's coming, of course, and she has bought a new hat, too. Must keep our end up with Litrik's family swanning around. Your aunts going?'

She had told him yes, and he had grunted. 'Gave them a bit of a shock, I dare say.' He patted her kindly on the shoulder. 'Well, you deserve a bit of the good life, Fran; you'll make a fine wife. Litrik's a lucky man.'

Litrik telephoned the next day, pleasantly brisk and businesslike. The date of the wedding was fixed, not quite three weeks away, and he would drive over three days before that and fetch her. Her aunts, he observed, would be taken care of by Tuggs, who would fetch them the day previous to the wedding and drive them back home again on the day following that. 'A short stay, I'm afraid,' he told her with no trace of apology, 'but I have an important conference in Brussels and there will be no chance to entertain them.'

'Do I have to tell them?'

She heard his quick impatient breath. 'I'll write to them. You have left the hospital?'

'Yes. Litrik, we are being married in church, aren't we?'

'Certainly. There is a civil wedding first, of course. The *dominee* is a personal friend of mine and he understands the situation. We will go and see him together. Cold feet?'

'Certainly not. How is Lisa?'

'In seventh heaven, bless her.' His voice warmed. 'She is really happy.'

Which made the whole thing worthwhile, reflected Fran as she wished him a rather sober goodbye.

She was neither impetuous nor impulsive; she spent the first day or so making lists and then took herself off to Bath, where she bought ivory satin, white tulle and fine lace and bore them off to the little woman who had made clothes for half the town for most of her life. If she was surprised to find that Fran wanted her wedding dress to be an exact copy of the mouse in the picture book she forbore from comment, but cut and stitched and fitted until an exact replica lay spread out in her workroom. When Fran went for a final fitting she allowed herself the observation that she had never expected the dress to turn out quite so exquisite. 'You'll look a treat, Miss Fran,' she declared. 'Mind you let me have a photo.'

There were other clothes to buy, of course, but first she had to drive the aunts to Bath so that they might purchase suitable finery. They had taken the news that they were to be fetched by Tuggs without too much argument, possibly because of the letter the doctor had written to them. Aunt Kate had been tart about the shortness of their visit to Holland, but, as Fran had pointed out with her usual common sense, he was a busy man and a prominent one in his profession and his work was very important to him.

Aunt Kate had sniffed. 'I suppose that, now you are to be married, we can no longer expect any care and attention; we three old ladies will have to manage as best we can.'

Fran stilled a rebellious tongue and took a deep calming breath. 'You are none of you old—why Miss Hawkins at the hospital is only a couple of years younger than you, Aunt Polly, and she works full time and housekeeps for her brother as well. And you forget that you have Winnie.'

'And that's another thing,' moaned Aunt Kate. 'Litrik insists that she should come to the wedding with us. I cannot think why.'

'I've known Winnie for years, Aunt Kate, she is my friend and Litrik knows that.' She added, with a touch of asperity, 'I'm taking her into Bath tomorrow to buy herself a hat.'

'I do not know what has come over you, Francesca. We have all said that you are a changed young woman.'

'I expect it's because I'm going to be married. I thought you would be pleased about that, Aunt.'

Aunt Kate looked uncomfortable. 'Of course we are pleased, but we had rather expected that you would stay here and look after us.'

'Well now I'll have a husband and a little step-daughter to look after instead,' observed Fran cheerfully. She dropped a kiss on her peevish aunt's cheek and went upstairs to try on three pairs of new shoes, a Jaeger suit, two crêpe de Chine dresses, a tweed skirt, a jersey dress with a wildly expensive belt and a handful of sweaters and blouses. She had spent a lot of money, but she had never felt the urge to buy many clothes before; there had been no reason to do so. She had always looked nice but unspectacular; now she had gathered together a wardrobe she hoped would be suitable for a doctor's wife. There was still money in the bank; right at the back of her mind was the dim thought that one day she might need it.

She wrote letters to Lisa, in English but interlarded with an occasional Dutch phrase. Litrik had been as good as his word. A rather formidable lady had telephoned to say that she had been requested to give Fran as many lessons in Dutch conversation as possible. She was a hard taskmaster, but, by the time Fran had packed her bags, said goodbye to her friends and organised her aunts' journey so that they would have no worries, she had learned a score of little sentences off by heart, and any number of everyday words. 'The grammar will have to be learned later,' her teacher had told her. 'At the moment you have none, but persevere with what you have learned and practise daily.

Your accent is tolerable and you can make yourself understood basically. I trust that Dr van Rijgen will be satisfied.'

'Oh, I am sure that he will,' declared Fran warmly. 'I can't thank you enough—I mean, Dutch doesn't sound like nonsense any more, if you know what I mean.'

She beamed at the lady, who found herself smiling back, at the same time wondering what Litrik van Rijgen could possibly see in such an ordinary girl. Nice eyes, pretty figure, sweet smile and a charming voice, but hardly scintillating.

He arrived exactly when he had said he would and was received by the aunts, sitting as they always did in their chairs in the drawing room. Fran, trotting to and fro between the kitchen and the dining room, hadn't heard the car. She opened the drawing room door and poked her head round it. 'Aunt Kate, Winnie wants some sherry for the soup...' She caught sight of the doctor, who had got to his feet at the sight of her, and went a little pink. 'Oh, you're here—hallo, Litrik.'

He crossed the room and put his hands on her shoulders and kissed her. 'I wondered where you were,' he remarked blandly. 'I supposed you to be in your room doing last minute things to your hair or something. Are you cooking the supper?'

The faint edge to his voice made the aunts wince. 'Winnie's doing that,' Aunt Polly hastened to say. 'Francesca always helps.'

He had kept an arm round her shoulders. 'Can Winnie spare you for ten minutes? I'm sure your aunts will forgive us if we have a short time together, perhaps in the garden? There are several small points to settle and we must leave early in the morning.'

He smiled gently. 'We might take the sherry with us and go through the kitchen…'

Fran took the bottle from the sideboard cupboard, reflecting that there was more to Litrik than she had thought; the aunts hadn't a chance. She gave him a shy smile, assured her aunts that they would be ten minutes, no more than that, and led the way out of the room. She was rather warm from the kitchen and her hair had escaped its neat bun; she didn't feel at her best, but on the other hand, Litrik had smiled at her like an old friend.

Winnie took the sherry, ushered them out through the kitchen door and told them severely that they'd better be back in ten minutes otherwise the chicken would be overdone.

In the soft evening light, Fran turned to look at him. 'Don't you like the aunts?' she asked.

'Charming ladies; also, as I have already said, selfish to their fingertips. Do you spend all your time in the kitchen?'

'No—oh no, but you see Winnie is not as young as she was and there are little jobs I can do to help.'

'And can your aunts not help occasionally?'

'They are not used to doing anything like that.'

He took her arm and strolled across the stretch of grass behind the house.

'No last minute misgivings?' he wanted to know.

'Only that I might not fit into your kind of life.'

He let that pass. 'You will find Lisa not quite as well as she was. I think that perhaps we were a little optimistic…'

She looked at him appalled. 'You mean, less than six months?'

'I'm afraid so.'

'I'm so sorry. I can't bear to think of it.'

'Then don't. Let us think instead of securing her a happy life while she is with us.'

'Oh, I promise that I will do that—anything…'

'She is in transports over her new dress—did you manage to get a dress resembling her story book mouse?'

She answered him seriously. 'Yes, down to the last button. No whiskers or tail of course!'

He smiled down at her and put a hand out to tuck away a strand of hair.

'But mousy hair in abundance. You'll be ready to leave by eight o'clock in the morning?'

'Yes. I have two cases and my wedding dress in a box. Will breakfast at just after seven suit you?'

'Very nicely. We say goodbye to the aunts this evening.'

'Well, yes; they don't like to be disturbed too early.'

'Then let us go and join them. Did I tell you that

Dr and Mrs Beecham will be driving over the day before the wedding? They'll be staying with us.'

'And the aunts?'

'Of course. The house is large enough. Nel is over the moon opening up the entire place.'

At the kitchen door, Fran paused. 'It'll work, won't it?' she asked him.

His voice was reassuringly warm. 'Oh, yes, Francesca, it will work.'

CHAPTER FOUR

IT was already warm when they left in the morning with Winnie to wave them goodbye. The aunts had been ready to bid them goodbye on the previous evening, managing to convey that although they were happy for Fran's future happiness they were themselves about to enter a period of deprivation caused by her permanent absence. Fran, remembering that as they drove away, felt vaguely guilty. She sat silently, wondering how her aunts would manage until Litrik spoke. 'Stop worrying, Francesca.' His voice was briskly friendly. 'Your aunts will manage very well; they do not really need you—they enjoyed making use of you. I am convinced that within a month we shall hear that they have found a suitable companion to take your place.'

He gave her a quick sideways smile which somehow reassured her. 'Now let us go over our plans for the next few days...'

A quite lengthy business which kept them occupied until they stopped for coffee. The hovercraft was full, for it was the height of the holiday season. Fran drank the coffee and ate the sandwiches which were brought to her and then sat quietly, not bothering to think, while Litrik, his briefcase open on his knees, wrote busily. He must have a great deal to do, she thought idly, but didn't pursue the thought; each time she had seen him he had appeared calm and unworried. She closed her eyes and nodded off on that reassuring thought.

They didn't stop again once they were on dry land and they were at the house as the clock on the dashboard showed the hour of five.

Litrik got out and came round to open her door. 'I've an hour,' he told her. 'We'll have tea, shall we, and then I'll have to leave you until about eight o'clock.'

He didn't wait for her answer for Tuggs was already coming down the steps to greet them and fetch the luggage. And, 'Welcome, Miss Manning,' he said warmly. 'We're all that glad to see you, and there's Lisa in such a state of excitement.'

'In the drawing room?' asked Litrik, and took Fran's arm as they went indoors.

The drawing room looked as lovely as she had remembered it, with the late afternoon sun pouring in and the soft colours of the furnishings glowing against its walls. And Lisa in her wheelchair, with faithful Nanny close by, her small face alight with excitement. The moment they went in she burst into talk and the doctor strode across the room and picked her up carefully and carried her to where Fran had hesitated.

'Mama,' shrieked Lisa and leaned from her father's arms to hug her. She broke into a babble of Dutch then and, obedient to a look from Litrik, Fran sat down and he put Lisa on her lap.

The child was thinner and paler although there was nothing in her manner to show that she wasn't as well as she had been. Fran glanced at Litrik in low-voiced talk with Nanny; he looked completely at ease and Nanny was smiling—perhaps he had become over-anxious… Fran settled down to one of the conversations she and Lisa so enjoyed, both understanding about half of what the other was saying and making up for the rest by a lot of giggling.

But soon Nel brought in the tea, smiling and nodding at Fran and shaking hands and presently Litrik came back and took Lisa on to his knees while Fran poured out.

'Nanny has gone to have her own tea; she'll be back presently so that you can unpack and rest if you want to. Dinner will be later than usual and Lisa will go to bed at her normal time. Tomorrow my family will arrive but not until lunchtime. I'll be at the hospital till about noon. And in the evening you and I are going to see the *dominee*.'

She had expected a busy few days before the wedding although the idea of meeting his family rather daunted her. Supposing they disliked her? And what about her clothes? It was still full summer and she had brought some pretty dresses with her as well as her new outfits. Would it be long dresses in the evening? She sat there, tell-tale thoughts worrying their way across her face.

'One thing at a time, Francesca,' said Litrik gently. 'Pour the tea, will you? Lisa wants to watch you unpack. Would you mind?'

'Of course not; in fact I'd like that very much.' She busied herself with the silver pot and the delicate china and joined in the cheerful talk about the wedding.

Nanny came back presently and Litrik went away, promising to look in on his small daughter when he got back home. His, 'Nel and Tuggs will look after you, Francesca,' were kindly uttered and she found it amusing that halfway to the door he remembered to come back and kiss her cheek.

She had wondered how she would fill in the time before he came home again but she need not have worried. Nanny wheeled Lisa's chair into the lift behind the staircase and, at a smile and a nod from Fran, left her in the large room which was to be hers. It was in the front of the house with a wide balcony. There was a bathroom and dressing room leading from it and it was furnished with beautifully polished pieces in yew and applewood. The floor was thickly carpeted and the three french windows were draped in old rose brocade, matching the spread on the bed. The dogs had joined them, sitting quietly side by side, satisfied now that they had got over the excitement of their master being back home.

Her cases had been unlocked and opened, both of them on a long chest against one wall, but the box with her wedding gown was unopened on the *chaise-*

longue at the foot of the bed. She opened that first because that was what Lisa wanted to see most. The little girl's gasps of delight as she spread the dress on the bed more than repaid her for the trouble she had taken over getting it just right. She wheeled the chair close to the bed so that Lisa might finger the material and examine every inch of it and then opened one of the cases and unwrapped the present she had brought. A mouse dressed in a miniature replica of her own wedding finery. It had been a fiddly business making the mouse and then dressing it, but, at the sight of Lisa's ecstatic face, she had no doubt that it had been worthwhile.

The unpacking was hilarious, for she had to describe each garment in English while Lisa strove to copy her and then insisted on teaching her the Dutch, and when Nanny came to fetch Lisa she was drawn into it, too. But presently Lisa was borne away for her supper and bed, which gave Fran the chance to have a leisurely bath and change into one of the thinner dresses, sitting to do her face with extra care and arrange her hair with her usual neatness. And by then it was time to go and say good night to Lisa, a protracted visit as it turned out for Lisa wished to be told a story.

'In English?' asked Fran, mentally surveying her small stock of Dutch phrases.

English it seemed would do very well; it had to be a long story, lasting for several nights and never mind if she couldn't understand any of it, and it had to concern one of Lisa's beloved mice.

Fran, who had a splendid imagination, began an involved tale, interlarded with the odd Dutch word and helped out by a wealth of hand waving and a variety of voices. She didn't hear or see Litrik come into the night nursery; she was sitting on the bed beside Lisa, quite carried away while Lisa sat enthralled. When he sat down on the bed beside her she came to a halt, feeling foolish, although Lisa broke at once into delighted chatter. He put an arm across Fran's back and took his daughter's hand in his and said something to quieten her, then, 'Do go on,' he begged, 'I always enjoyed a good fairy story.'

'Well, that's the end actually; it's in instalments you see.' She felt shy and a bit silly.

'Then I must be sure and hear the second part.' He said something to Lisa and made her laugh and Fran got up and bent to kiss the child good night. The doctor did the same and the child tugged at his arm.

'It seems you are to be kissed, too,' he murmured to Fran and brushed her cheek lightly.

Fran caught sight of the child's eager little face watching them: she leaned up and kissed him with considerable warmth and felt his quick surprised breath.

They ate dinner, a delicious meal, at an elegantly laid table, the doctor completely at ease and Fran, outwardly at least, her usual calm self. They talked of this and that, made no mention of the wedding and discussed the weather. No one, thought Fran, spooning the luscious sorbet Tuggs had put before her, would know, just seeing us here like this, that we are going to be married in three days time. She glanced up and found his eyes upon her and blushed guiltily as though she had spoken her thoughts aloud.

Tuggs had gone to fetch the coffee and take it to the drawing room when Litrik said blandly, 'We'll have to do better than this, won't we? Do you suppose we might forget our true feelings towards each other and pretend that we at least like one another? It will get easier once we start. Supposing we go to the drawing room and discuss the wedding like two old friends? In fact, could we not regard the whole exercise as an undertaking agreed upon between two people with one object in mind, to keep Lisa happy?'

Fran poured the coffee and handed him his cup. She said slowly, 'I've been selfish, I'm sorry—let's start again.'

'That's generous of you, Francesca, for the blame is mine; I have rushed you along without giving you time to, er—get into the part.'

He smiled at her with a charm to put her instantly at ease.

'Your family?' she asked him. 'I'm scared of meeting them, you know. I mean, do they think that we're...well, that you wanted to marry me?'

'I have told them that I have found the girl I want as a wife. That's true enough, isn't it? I am not a man to show my feelings too often and they wouldn't expect it.'

'And me?' Fran ignored grammar in her anxiety to get the matter clear. 'And what about my feelings?'

'I am sure that you will act your part admirably, Francesca. Shall we consider ourselves partners? I give you my word that I will do all in my power to make life easy for you.'

'And your friends?'

'They will come to the reception after our wedding, possibly we shall be invited out to dinner or drinks from time to time, but that should present no difficulties for you. You realise that your days will be largely taken up with Lisa?' He added bleakly, 'I very much doubt if she will be with us for Christmas.'

Christmas, from the viewpoint of early August, seemed a long way off. All the same Fran gave a little shiver. 'There is always hope.'

He didn't answer that. 'I have arranged to see Ivo Meertens, the *dominee,* after tea tomorrow. He understands the situation perfectly; you can say anything you like to him, ask him any questions, voice any doubts. We will go to his house and you can be sure that anything you say to him will go no further.'

'He—he does approve of what we are doing?'

'Yes. You see, Francesca, we are not hurting anyone, neither of us is emotionally involved, neither of us is hurting the other. On the other hand, we are making Lisa's remaining months happy ones.'

'I accept that,' she told him seriously. 'I promise

you I will do my best to make Lisa happy.' Suddenly
it was all a bit too much. She mumbled, 'Do you mind
if I say good night? I'm tired…'

He got to his feet at once. 'Of course, it's been a
long day. I breakfast at eight o'clock if you like to
join me, but if you would rather, your breakfast will
be brought to you in bed.'

'In bed? I can't remember when I had breakfast in
bed. I'd rather have it here with you, Litrik.'

'Splendid.' He walked with her to the door and
opened it and as she went past him stopped her for a
moment with a hand. 'Good night,' he said and kissed
her gently.

She had meant to go over the day's happenings in
the peace and quiet of her bed but she was asleep the
moment her head touched the pillow. In the morning,
sitting up in bed drinking the tea Nel had brought her,
there seemed no reason to do so. Besides if she was
to have breakfast with Litrik she would have to get
up and dress.

The faint lingering doubt that his friendliness and
warmth of manner of the previous evening might have
reverted to his usual chilly politeness was dispelled
when she got downstairs, and she gave a small relieved sigh as he got up from his place at the table,
wished her good morning and begged her to help herself to whatever she wished.

Breakfast was in a small room behind the dining
room, with a round table and pretty rosewood chairs,
a sideboard upon which were several covered dishes,

and a wide window overlooking the garden. The sun streamed in making everything warm and bright and normal. Fran settled down to a good breakfast, all her overnight fears banished.

'Lunch will be at one o'clock.' Litrik's voice broke into her thoughts. 'Mother and the family will arrive about half past twelve; I shall be home by then.' He got up ready to leave. 'Have a happy morning with Lisa.' And since Tuggs had come into the room he paused by her chair and kissed her.

The morning passed quickly, walking round the garden with Lisa and Nanny; there was no lack of conversation even if it was a bit muddled. With Lisa borne away for her rest Fran hurried to her room and took an anxious look at her person in the pier-glass. She had put on a cotton dress in leaf green with a wide white collar and soft leather belt round her slim waist. There was nothing more she could do about her face and hair, she decided. She went back downstairs and wandered into the drawing room and found Litrik there.

Her, 'Oh, good, you are back,' was uttered with a warmth quite unlike her usual calm voice and he said, 'Nervous? You don't need to be. Have you had a pleasant morning?'

He was so casual that she bit back all the things she wanted to say. 'Very nice, thank you,' she told him.

He crossed the room and stood in front of her,

picked up her left hand and slid a ring on to her finger. 'My grandmother's—I'm glad to see that it fits.'

She looked at the sparkling diamond surrounded by sapphires in an old fashioned gold setting, and then at him, a question in her eyes.

'No—Lisa's mother had no interest in the family jewellery, but I fancy that perhaps you will like it?'

'Oh, I do, it's so beautiful. Thank you very much, Litrik.' Rather awkwardly she lifted her face to his and kissed his cheek. She had wondered once or twice about a ring but now she was taken by surprise. She was bewildered by the sudden urge to burst into tears for no reason at all. Well, there was a reason; he had given it to her with a casualness which made a mockery of the giving. But what else was there to expect? She said quietly, 'I shall take great care of it while I am wearing it.' For, of course, she would return it within a few months...

There was the sound of a car driving up to the door and he said, 'Shall we go and meet my mother and father?'

She had no need to be nervous; his father was an elderly edition of himself, white haired, self-assured and with a warmth in his manner which Litrik lacked, and his mother was splendidly tall, beautifully dressed, with a face which had no pretentions to good looks and the kindest of smiles.

They greeted her with a pleasure she hadn't expected and his mother said at once, 'We are so happy to have you in the family, my dear, and I speak for everyone. There are rather a lot of us but don't let us overwhelm you.' She twinkled nicely at Fran. 'When we have a few minutes to ourselves we will go somewhere quiet and have a good gossip.'

Her English was faultless. Fran smiled rather shyly, 'I shall like that,' and found that Litrik had taken her hand while they were talking.

'Lisa is over the moon,' he told his mother. 'The two of them had an instant rapport.' He broke off at the sound of voices in the hall. 'The family,' he observed and flung an arm round Fran's shoulders. She needed it; her knees were wobbling with fright.

To Fran, who had no family other than her three aunts and Clare, the steady stream of aunts, uncles, cousins, nephews and nieces was quite bewildering. Litrik, standing at her elbow, meticulously introduced her to each and every one of them and she smiled and shook hands and kissed cheeks and forgot their names immediately. One or two of them stood out from the rest: Great Uncle Timon, a giant of an old man with a splendid head of white hair and a fierce moustache and a command of English which left her blinking. And the two aunts from Friesland, Tante Olda and Tante Nynke, formidable in elegant black dresses, gold chains draping their splendid bosoms, leaning over her from their superior height and, surprisingly, positively motherly towards her. There were children, too, well behaved and polite and palpably relieved when they were sent into the garden to play, taking Nanny and Lisa with them. There were perhaps twenty-five people there although it seemed at least twice that number. It was a mercy that they all spoke English with an ease she envied; there had been no need for her to have worked so hard at her Dutch lessons before she had left home for there would be no chance to air what little knowledge she had. Anyway, she would be terrified to try it out on these self-assured relations, even though they were behaving so kindly towards her.

She gave a little shiver; she was a fraud and it was all wrong that everyone should be so bent on making her feel that she was one of the family.

Litrik, chatting to a thick-set middle-aged man whom she vaguely identified as Uncle Hilwert, felt the shiver and drew her a little closer. He said lightly, 'Uncle Hilwert is anxious that we should have a large family. He was the eldest of ten children and he has six sons and daughters, all married.' He glanced down at her, smiling easily. 'We must do our best, mustn't we, Francesca?'

She managed a smile, trying to imagine Litrik surrounded by half a dozen children. Of course, he was marvellous with Lisa but then she was just one child and a very sick one to boot. Six all bursting with childish health presented rather a different picture. She had gone a little pink and given Litrik a quick look and found him still smiling.

Uncle Hilwert was joined by Litrik's sisters, Jebbeke and Wilma, who wanted to talk about the wedding. Fran liked them; they were friendly, anxious to

put her at her ease and, at the same time, didn't fire
questions at her. They teased Litrik gently and then
carried her off to join a group of younger cousins.

'You can have Fran back presently,' declared
Wilma cheerfully. 'After all you'll have her for the
rest of your life and that's years and years…'

He let her go at once with some laughing remark
and she wondered if he felt as bad about it as she did.
She must stop thinking like that, she reminded herself
as she crossed the room with Wilma and Jebbeke. She
had promised that she would fulfil her side of their
bargain and that was all that mattered. The circle of
cousins opened out to absorb her and it wasn't until
they had had their drinks and Tuggs had announced
lunch that Litrik came looking for her.

They sat side by side with Lisa squeezed in between them. The little girl didn't say much; she ate
her lunch carefully and, as Fran saw with some disquiet, with no appetite, but every now and then a
small hand crept into hers and gave it a squeeze. Lisa
at least was happy.

There was a general move into the gardens after
they had had coffee, the grown ups strolling around,
going from group to group, the children milling
around happily, taking it in turns to sit with Lisa.

'Happy, darling?' asked Fran, sitting down beside
her on the grass near to her chair. Lisa beamed at her.
'Happy,' she echoed. She had the mouse bride
clutched under one arm and she was a little flushed.
Fran sat quietly, for the child was tired; she took a

small hand in hers and said, 'Go to sleep, darling,' and Lisa, understanding her, closed her eyes. Nanny, ever watchful, nodded and smiled at Fran, and wheeled the chair carefully into the house.

Litrik slid down on to the grass beside her. For such a large man he was remarkably light on his feet. If she had expected him to have made some soothing or encouraging remark, she was mistaken. All he said was, 'This isn't too good for Lisa, but she had set her heart on it, and she is happy. Do you like my family?'

'Very much.' If he could talk in that rather offhand way, so could she. 'They've all been very kind…'

He turned two suddenly cold eyes upon her. 'Naturally. You are to be my wife and I am the head of the family.'

She said tartly, 'Oh, I had hoped that they liked me for myself, not because I was marrying you.'

He smiled; the slow mocking smile she remembered so well from his lectures when some unfortunate nurse had given him a silly answer to his question.

'Do not allow such nonsense to cloud your common sense, Francesca, but, if it will allay your fears, I assure you that, to a man, the family have taken you to their hearts.'

'I am glad to hear it. They must have been surprised; I don't think I'm at all what they expected…'

'What should they have expected?' he asked idly.

'Well, someone tall and willowy and fair, beautifully dressed and used to living in large houses.'

He said abruptly, 'They are two a penny, Francesca; you are unique.'

She wanted to ask him what he meant by that but his mother and the two aunts from Friesland bore down upon them and he whisked her to her feet and gave her a little push. 'Mother's dying to see your dress; you'd better satisfy her curiosity, my dear.'

She took the three ladies into the house and up to her bedroom and displayed her wedding gown and felt pleased at their admiration. 'You will be a pretty bride, my dear,' declared Mevrouw van Rijgen. 'You are so small and slender. You will not mind living in Holland?'

'Of course, she won't,' observed Tante Olda in a shocked voice. 'She will be happy wherever Litrik is. This is his home and now it will be hers.'

Mevrouw van Rijgen eased her feet out of her elegant pumps. 'Nevertheless, life will be different, I'm sure. Litrik has a great many friends and there will be entertaining. You will, I am sure, Francesca, be a delightful hostess and a splendid wife to Litrik—not the easiest of men,' she added with a twinkle. 'What is he like as a doctor? I have often wondered but how could I ask him?'

'He is a splendid doctor; the patients like him; they trust him, too, and that means a lot…'

'And the nurses, do they like him, too?'

Fran smiled. 'Oh, yes, but only from a distance, if you see what I mean; he is—well, he is a bit intimidating without knowing it.'

'He doesn't intimidate you?' queried Tante Nynke. Fran shook her head. 'No, not in the least.'

'You are a calm girl,' stated her future mother-in-law, 'and an ideal wife for Litrik.' She got up and made her stately way in her stockinged feet to where Fran was sitting on the dressing-table stool. 'I am so very happy to have you for my third daughter, my dear.'

She kissed Fran's cheek and, for the second time that day, Fran wanted to cry. Here was someone she could learn to love, an ideal mother-in-law, and within a few months she would never see her again. Her pact with Litrik which had seemed so straightforward was getting out of hand.

They had tea scattered round the drawing room, with Lisa sitting on her father's knee. Probably the happiest person in the room, reflected Fran, listening politely to Great Uncle Timon booming the van Rijgen family history into her ear. She was rescued by Litrik.

'Time we paid our visit to Dominee Meertens,' he observed and whisked her out the room with the remark that they would be back in good time for dinner. Fran went to drop a kiss on Lisa's small cheek as they departed. *'Tot ziens,'* she whispered and Lisa giggled and answered with the 'bye, bye' Fran had taught her.

There were two cars at the door, the Daimler with Thor and Muff sitting patiently inside it, and a dark blue Bristol with Tugg's head inside its bonnet.

'Tugg's leaving in a few minutes to collect your aunts,' observed Litrik. 'He'll leave the car at Schiphol and fly over—there will be a car waiting for him at Heathrow. He'll drive down, spend the night at an inn and fetch your aunts in the morning. They'll be here by tea time tomorrow.'

They walked over to the Bristol and Tuggs withdrew his head to say, 'Just off, sir. Nel's got everything in hand. I should be back with the ladies by four or five o'clock tomorrow.'

'Good. Get a decent night's sleep, Tuggs. Wim will be in to clean the cars and do any odd chores so take a couple of hours off when you get back here. Nel's got enough help in the kitchen and house?'

'Ample, sir. Never had so many willing helpers—there's nothing like a wedding…'

He beamed at them both and Litrik opened the Daimler's doors, urged Fran into the front seat, whistled to the dogs in the back and drove to the village.

The *dominee*'s house was by the church, an austere red brick edifice with square windows, a neat front garden and a half-open door. The *dominee* appeared at the door as they got out and as they reached it they heard a subdued confusion of sounds; someone was doing five finger exercises on a piano, children's voices were raised in fierce argument, a dog was barking, and someone, somewhere, was singing with more noise than talent. The *dominee,* probably inured to such domestic sounds, took no notice of them but merely raised his voice a little.

'Come in, Litrik.' He shook hands and turned to Fran. 'And this is Francesca.' He wrung her hand. 'Just as you described, too. The study will be the best place for our talk. My wife will bring coffee and then we can talk.'

His English was fluent but heavily accented and he had a booming voice which Fran considered might be of great advantage in church.

His study was a dark room, full of books, a massive desk taking up one corner. He waved them to chairs and when his wife came in with the coffee tray introduced her to Fran. She was a tall young woman with ash blonde hair and blue eyes. She shook hands with Fran, kissed Litrik and said in awkward English, 'Later when the wedding is over, we must become friends.'

'I'd like that,' said Fran, taking an instant liking to her. She saw her go with regret; the *dominee* was a bit overpowering and Litrik... She wished she knew him better.

She poured the coffee when she was asked to and sat drinking it while the two men discussed some knotty problem concerning the village hall. But presently they put their cups down and the *dominee* leaned back in his chair and addressed her.

'Litrik has told you that I am aware of your reasons for marrying. We discussed it at some length when he first decided to ask you to be his wife. His reasons, unusual though they are, are sound and compassionate and I have no doubt that you agreed to marry him for those reasons. You must dispel any doubts you may have, Francesca; you are hurting no one; you are bringing a great deal of happiness to Lisa for the last few months of her life. The fact that there is no emotional tie between the two of you ensures its success. You are, as it were, working together as you would to cure a ward full of patients, only in this case it is a small child.'

He had got up as he had been speaking and was pacing up and down the room. Now he stopped in front of her, frowning fiercely. 'Have I made myself clear? Your marriage will be as sincere as any other which I have performed; that it is undertaken for the reasons of which I have spoken is a secret between the three of us.'

Fran felt a bit overpowered; this, she felt, was only half-strength; she wondered what one of his sermons would be like when he could employ the full thunder of his voice. Yet she liked him; he was sincere and, she felt sure, fearless, and there was no denying that he had dispelled any doubts that might have been lurking. She looked at Litrik and saw that he was watching her intently.

'I don't think that I had any doubts, but I've not really had the time to think about that. I'm grateful and relieved that you agree with what we are doing and that we'll have your support. There is just one thing…' She cast the doctor an apologetic look. 'When we—when we no longer need to be married, will it be possible to annul our marriage quickly and

quietly? Litrik has already told me that it shouldn't
be a problem but I was thinking about his family.'
She turned her shoulder to Litrik so that she couldn't
see his face. 'They have been more than kind to me
and accepted me...' She added fiercely, 'I'm not being saintly or anything like that, but I don't want them
hurt or Litrik's career ruined.'

Litrik was staring at the back of her head from
under lowered lids. 'What about your own career?'

'You said you'd see that I got a job,' she mumbled
over her shoulder.

'So I did. I know that Dominee Meertens will reassure you about the annulment, just as I can reassure
you that my career won't suffer in the least and we
shall do the best we can, the pair of us, not to upset
the family.' His voice was suddenly harsh. 'Marriages
go on the rocks, you know. What has happened once
can easily happen for a second time. Only we shall I
hope part without rancour.'

'Remember Lisa,' said the *dominee* suddenly.
'Nothing is quite as important as her happiness.'

'No—no, of course not.' Fran studied the *dominee*'s face; he was a fierce man but a very good one.
She smiled at him. 'While we are here, could you tell
me if the service is very different to ours; my cousin
who is married to a Dutchman wrote and described it
to me, but it was all a bit vague.'

He beamed back at her. 'Ah, of course. This calls
for more coffee and Siska.' He opened the door and
raised his voice above the various noises coming from

round the house, and when his wife appeared gave her the coffee tray. She was back within minutes and sat down by Fran and poured out and presently she and the *dominee* described the service between them.

'You know about the civil ceremony first?' asked the *dominee*.

'Oh, yes. Litrik explained.'

'Good. So you see that the ceremony is simple and short. The difference is that he will come with you to the church. You have bridesmaids?'

'No—you see Lisa can't be one…'

He nodded. 'Of course. It will be a happy occasion for her and for all of us.'

She and Litrik got up to go presently. They had nothing to say until he stopped the car in front of his own door but then Fran, unable to contain herself any longer, asked, 'Why didn't you say something? Why did you just sit there? You let Dominee Meertens do all the talking…'

'My dear Francesca, I had already stated my case. What was needed was a third party to give an unbiased opinion.'

'And just supposing he had opposed the whole thing? He might have changed his mind…'

'Which answers your question.' He got out and opened her door and took her arm as they went up the steps. Just in case someone was watching from the house, Fran thought peevishly.

They went together to say good night to Lisa and

as they went down the staircase Fran paused halfway. 'Will everyone be dressed up?' she wanted to know.

'I imagine so. Eve of the wedding isn't it, more or less? Tomorrow there will be another dinner party but this evening is rather special—your welcome into the family.' He added kindly, 'Worried about what you will wear?'

'Well yes. I've only some summer dresses with me and some things I bought for later on. There is a skirt and top though…I don't want to let you down.'

'You would never do that. Supposing I got Wilma or Jebbeke to come along to your room presently?'

'Oh, thanks—they could tell me if I had the right things.'

The top and skirt were pronounced just the thing and indeed, surveying her person in the long wall mirror, she had to admit that they did something for her. Litrik, coming across the room to meet her when she got downstairs, bent to kiss her cheek and murmured, 'Charming, my dear. Did you show yourself to Lisa?'

She nodded, smiling shyly, feeling relief.

The evening was a thumping success; dinner, elaborate and beautifully served, took up the greater part of the evening and afterwards the younger members of the party rolled back the silken rugs in the drawing room and danced.

Fran, who loved dancing and did it well, took to the floor with Litrik and presently everyone was dancing.

Her sleepy head on the pillow, she reflected with

surprise that she was happier than she had ever been in her life; she wasn't sure how that was possible when she remembered Lisa, excepting that the little girl was happy, too. She smiled at the memory of the child's excited little face and the small delicate hand tucked into hers. Fran closed her eyes, her last thought of Litrik's light kiss brushing her cheek as they had said good night. Most of the family had been there watching, which was why he had kissed her; all the same it had been nice.

The lovely weather held. Litrik was called away to an emergency at the hospital during the morning and Fran took Lisa for a walk in her chair while the older ladies went to supervise the flower arrangements in the church. Litrik was back for lunch and they all scattered into the grounds of the house afterwards to sit about and gossip. But as they left the table Litrik had taken her arm, saying, 'You haven't seen the house yet, have you? We'll go round now.'

It had taken most of the afternoon; the drawing room, the dining room, a dear little parlour at the back of the house, Litrik's study, a billiard room and several small rooms used for mending and sewing and doing the flowers. Upstairs there were seemingly endless bedrooms, all of them beautifully furnished with bathrooms cunningly fitted into corners and most of them with balconies. There was a floor above, too. 'The nurseries,' explained Litrik in a disinterested voice, 'and more guest rooms. There is another floor above this one. Tuggs and his wife live there, and the maids.'

Fran, following him obediently from room to room, could think of nothing to say.

The aunts arrived at tea time and she bore them away to their rooms to tidy themselves and listen to their account of the journey. A most rewarding experience, they told her, they had been taken the greatest care of by Tuggs. The car had been comfortable and, since no mishap had occurred during their flight to Schiphol, they were willing to concede that flying was a pleasant mode of travel.

She led them down to the drawing room for tea and was relieved when Litrik took charge, introducing them to each member of the family and settling them finally with the two aunts from Friesland and his mother.

Dinner that evening was as elaborate as on the previous evening but there was no dancing afterwards. The civil ceremony was at ten o'clock on the following morning and everyone would have to be up reasonably early.

The party broke up soon after eleven o'clock and Fran, having escorted her aunts to their rooms and wished them good night, went soft footed to take a last look at Lisa. The child was asleep and there was no denying the fact that her small face looked pinched and white. Fran went to her room, undressed and got into bed. At least, she reminded herself, Lisa was going to be happy for a few months.

She woke early in another glorious morning, too lovely to stay in bed. She nipped to the window and pulled back the curtains and opened the door on to the balcony. It was quiet except for the birds; she leaned her elbows on the railing and took stock of the garden below and then became aware that Litrik was standing under the copper beech beyond the lawn. He had the dogs with him and was wearing slacks and an open-necked shirt.

'Come on down,' he urged her. 'We can have a few minutes' peace and quiet before we're engulfed.'

Fran tossed her mane of mousy hair over her shoulders, suddenly aware of wearing nothing but her nightie. 'All right, I'll be five minutes.'

Slacks and a top would do; she thrust her feet into sandals, washed her face and tied back her hair and trod quietly through the sleeping house.

He was waiting by the open front door, the dogs pacing to and fro, anxious not to miss their walk.

Litrik said without preamble. 'This is your last chance, Francesca. You're still willing to go through with it?'

She fell into step beside him, the dogs bustling around the pair of them. She had never been so sure of anything in her whole life before, although she didn't quite know why.

'I'm quite sure,' she told him in a steady voice. 'I went to look at Lisa last night before I went to bed— she looked so pale and ill. I'll not let her look like that…'

He tucked her hand under his arm. 'I beg your pardon for asking you that, Francesca. You are not one to back out of a promise, are you? Between us both we'll keep her happy.'

They turned back towards the house and saw Tuggs coming towards them.

'There's your early morning tea,' he told them and then, accusingly, 'you didn't ought to be seeing each other before you are wed.' He sounded severe. 'Unlucky, some say.' He added hastily, 'Not that you'll be unlucky, sir and miss.'

Litrik laughed and clapped him on the shoulders. 'Indeed we won't, Tuggs. Let's have some of that tea, shall we? Is everything going well?'

'Bless you, yes, sir. Nel's got everyone organised.'

He left them to drink their tea then and presently Fran said in a matter-of-fact voice, 'Well, I'll see you later,' and sped away to take a bath and have a good breakfast in her room as time-honoured custom dictated.

CHAPTER FIVE

LISA came to watch her dress and various cousins and aunts and Litrik's mother paid admiring visits. 'Delightful,' pronounced Mevrouw van Rijgen. 'That is the prettiest dress—how proud Litrik must be, my dear.'

Fran murmured a nothing; she thought it very unlikely that he was even interested enough to notice what she was wearing, although presently, when everyone had left for the *raadhuis* and she went downstairs to the hall where Litrik was waiting for her, she felt a thrill of pleasure at his look of surprised admiration. He handed her her bouquet and they went together to where the Daimler, its windows wreathed with flowers, stood waiting with Tuggs, spruce and sporting a buttonhole.

'Now there's a sight for sore eyes,' he told them happily. 'I never saw a handsomer pair.'

Fran smiled at him. No one could call her handsome, although Litrik in morning suit and top hat fitted that description. Indeed, he looked to be every girl's dream of a husband; it seemed most unfair that he was, so to speak, to be wasted on her. But only for a few months, she reminded herself soberly.

There was a small crowd outside the *raadhuis* and

the wedding chamber inside was packed. She saw Lisa, right in front with Nanny, and Dr and Mrs Beecham and her aunts and Litrik's parents; the rest was a blur of faces. The ceremony was short and when the ring was put on her finger she didn't feel in the least married. She signed her name obediently, received her marriage book and left the *raadhuis* on Litrik's arm, to get back into the car and be driven the short distance to the church.

Dominee Meertens was waiting for them there and this time things made sense; now she felt well and truly married. She glanced up at Litrik's face as they turned to go down the aisle and found him smiling; he would be happy now, she thought, because Lisa would be happy, too. The smile was really for her but that was to be expected. She must remember what Dominee Meertens had said: they were working together for the child's happiness.

They went down the aisle followed by the family and a great many people she supposed were friends of Litrik's. Almost at the door she saw Clare and Karel smiling and waving and she smiled back; they would be at the reception presently and she would be able to talk to them, perhaps invite them over for a day… There were more people outside the church now, as well as photographers and guests showering them with confetti and rose petals. Fran smiled and smiled and got into the car at last with Litrik beside her, her bouquet clutched in one hand, the other, with the gold wedding ring, on her silken lap.

She sought in vain for something to say; what did newly wed people say to each other? Or perhaps they just held hands, too happy to speak… It was a relief when Litrik said lightly, 'Well you should feel well and truly married, my dear, twice over.'

'Yes, well actually, I didn't feel awfully married at the civil ceremony. But I liked the church service. How pretty Lisa looked in that pink dress.'

It was easier after that; they talked about the reception and the number of guests who would be coming and the unfortunate manner in which Great Uncle Timon had blown his nose so violently during the prayers. By the time they reached the house, Fran had recovered almost all of her normal calm and when the first of the family arrived, she was standing in the drawing room by the open doors leading to the gardens, with Litrik beside her, looking composed and almost pretty in her wedding finery.

For the next few hours she lived in a kind of mosaic of voices and laughter, eye-catching hats, champagne and a seemingly never ending stream of people offering congratulations. Clare, radiant in yards of flowered chiffon, kissed her warmly.

'Darling, you look lovely. What a day—gosh, you must be over the moon!' She glanced around her. 'This gorgeous house, and I've never seen so much heavenly food. Is he very rich?'

Fran glanced at Litrik's broad back turned a little away from them while he talked to Dr Beecham. 'I expect so.' A reply which puzzled her cousin.

The aunts, determinedly British amongst so many foreigners, nonetheless assured her that they were re-assured by the undoubted respectability of Litrik's family and friends, and confessed that they were enjoying themselves. 'It is a pity that our stay is to be so short,' commented Aunt Kate, 'but we do realise that Litrik is a busy man. We hope that you will pay us a visit before very long.'

Aunt Janet sighed. 'It is a pity about the little girl. She has a splendid Nanny, I am told.'

'Yes everyone loves her and she is always happy...'

'She seems to like you,' Aunt Kate sounded doubtful.

'We are both fond of each other. She is my little daughter now...'

Litrik had turned back to her; she felt his hand tighten on her arm, and when she looked at him he was smiling. 'Our Lisa is very precious to us isn't she, my dear?'

Aunt Kate, who prided herself on plain speaking, observed sharply, 'Such a pity that she is an invalid. Will she get better?'

Fran didn't wait for Litrik; she said impulsively, 'Of course she will. She has the very best of treatment.'

'Naturally,' declared Aunt Kate drily, 'with an eminent physician for her father.'

Only Litrik's hand on her arm stopped Fran from speaking her mind at that. He said smoothly, 'I am sure you would like to see round the gardens.' He had caught the eye of a youngish cousin, who made his way towards them. 'Lucas, Francesca's aunts haven't seen the rose garden. Would you like to take them there?'

It was Aunt Polly, who hadn't spoken at all, who lingered behind for a moment to whisper, 'I'm sorry, my dears,' before hurrying away to catch up.

They were surrounded by guests at once. There was no chance to say anything and after that there were the toasts, and since Fran was English a wedding cake to cut, and then more guests.

But presently, after the tea and cakes brought round by the waiters, everyone but the family took their leave. Mevrouw van Rijgen took off her hat and her shoes and settled on one of the sofas, the older ladies sank thankfully into comfortable chairs, the men went off to the billiard room and the young ones went out into the garden. There was to be a family dinner party and directly after that everyone would leave. Fran found it strange but when she mentioned it to Litrik he said blandly, 'But my dear, of course we are to be left alone; your aunts are to stay with my mother and father, Tuggs will go over and drive them home tomorrow.'

He took her arm. 'Let's go for a stroll and take Lisa with us?'

'Like this?' she said, looking down at her satin-clad person.

'Why not? You have to wear your wedding gown until the last guest has gone.'

'Oh, do I? Then let's go into the gardens—Lisa is looking tired, bless her! perhaps we could sit somewhere quiet for a while and she might doze.'

They sat under the mulberry tree, the three of them, not talking, and no one bothered them until it was time for Lisa to go to bed. Fran wheeled her round while she said good night to everyone and then handed her over to Nanny and said, 'Yes, I will come and say good night,' to the girl, knowing that she understood that.

'Papa?' asked Lisa.

'And Papa.'

They went upstairs together presently, she and Litrik, and sat on the small bed talking quietly about the wedding until the child's eyes closed.

Outside in the corridor, Fran said, 'I'll go and tidy myself ready for dinner.'

He gave her a casual glance. 'You look all right,' he told her and her bosom swelled with indignation. Brides didn't look all right, they looked lovely or charming or even beautiful. She turned away to cross the gallery above the stairs but he stopped her. 'Just a minute. Lisa expects to have her morning tea with us—I'll tell Nel to see that it's taken to your room and—I'll join you there.' He grinned, looking years younger. 'If you remember in the picture book of hers, Mama and Papa Mouse take tea together with rows of small mice tucked in between them.'

She was still smarting from his casual acceptance of her appearance. She said haughtily, 'I have already told you that I will help you in any way to make Lisa happy.' She opened her door and whisked through it before she would let him see the tears in her eyes. The day had been a happy one until now, she had actually felt married to Litrik, sure that they would be able to live together as friends, even enjoy each other's company, but now she wasn't so sure. She was just a means to an end, to keep Lisa happy for a few months; he didn't think of her as a person at all; he was a cold-hearted, autocratic, hateful man, and he hadn't changed one iota from the sarcastic egotistical lecturer of her student days.

She did her face and rearranged her veil and then went on to the balcony. The August day was fading into a soft glow and the gardens were quiet now. She would have liked to have stayed there but they might think it strange if she didn't join them. She went down to the drawing room and Litrik crossed the room and took her hand. 'Here you are, my dear. A champagne cocktail before we go in to dinner?' And he stayed with her, going from group to group, suave and charming. He should have been an actor, reflected Fran, whose drink had gone straight to her head.

Dinner, served a little earlier than usual so that everyone could get home that night, was magnificent: oysters, smoked salmon, devilled crab or creamed kipper fillets, followed by fillets of sole bonne femme and then crown roast of lamb or wild duck with black cherry sauce and finally trifle and a pavlova cake with a pear and raspberry filling. Fran, who had eaten only a couple of the tempting morsels served at the reception, enjoyed every mouthful, the whole having been helped along nicely by the champagne. It was a merry meal with a great deal of talk and laughter, but at the end of it, when everyone had gone back to the drawing room for coffee, the goodbyes were begun. Litrik's parents were the first to leave, followed by the rest of the family. Some of them were driving back to Friesland and as the last of them disappeared down the drive Fran asked, 'Did they have to go? Surely they could have stayed the night and gone in the morning?'

Litrik had turned to her with the faintly mocking smile she disliked so much. 'My dear girl—on our wedding night? An unheard of thing!'

She had blushed and walked away from him, back into the drawing room, suddenly feeling lonely. Even the aunts would have been company but they had kissed her good night and wished her well with a faint air of self-pity; they would miss her, they said, and Litrik, overhearing Aunt Polly's comment that they would have to manage as best they could now, allowed himself a smile.

He had followed her into the drawing room. 'Breakfast at the usual time?' he asked her. 'With Lisa, of course. I've a full day's work tomorrow but I should be home by tea time. I'm sure you and Lisa will find plenty to do.'

She turned to face him. 'Oh, yes, we've so many plans... It was a very nice day.' She paused, it seemed rather a lukewarm way of describing one's wedding day but he, at least, hadn't even called it that. She would have to go to bed content with the fact that she had looked all right.

She said abruptly. 'Good night, Litrik,' and turned and flew up the stairs and into her splendid bedroom, where she undressed very fast and then spent far too long in a hot bath, having a good cry. He could have said something nice even if it wasn't true. After all it had been her wedding day. His family and friends had been sweet and admired her dress and said how pretty she had looked. She hadn't quite believed them but it had been nice to hear, all the same. She got into bed at last with a headache from too much champagne and crying, and then got out again to creep along the corridor to take a look at Lisa. There was a night light by her bed and she looked small and frail by its dim light. Fran turned and went back to her room, pausing to look over the gallery to the hall below. The house was quiet, although there were lights below. As she stood there she saw the study door open and Litrik came out and close the door behind him. She bolted back into her own room then and leapt into bed and turned out the lamps, which when she thought about it was silly and quite unnecessary.

She slept, although she hadn't thought she would, to be wakened by Nel with her early morning tea and a minute later a tap on the door and Nanny carrying Lisa, pink cheeked and eyes sparkling.

Nanny, settling her carefully beside Fran, said softly, 'Good morning, Mevrouw. There is fever this morning, will you tell the doctor?'

Fran nodded, 'Yes, of course, Nanny. He'll want to see you?'

'I think yes, Mevrouw.' Nanny slipped away and Fran lent an ear to Lisa's happy chatter, understanding most of it. When there was a knock on the door and Litrik came in in his dressing-gown she stared at him open-mouthed and then remembered that he was to have his tea each morning *en famille* because that was what Lisa expected. His good morning was cheerful and he bent to brush her cheek before sitting down on the bed beside his daughter, embarking on a long conversation with her while Fran poured the tea, but presently he asked in English, 'You slept well?'

'Yes, thank you.' She wondered why he looked at her so intently, unaware that her nose was pink as were her eyelids from crying. She handed him a biscuit and after a moment offered him more tea.

'I must say this is a pleasant way in which to begin the day. Very domestic.'

'Yes. Nanny wants to see you before you go.'

He nodded calmly. 'Yes, I can see why. A quiet day if you can manage it, Francesca. There are several pleasant walks round here if you feel like it. If you can manage the chair down to the lake you could sit there—she loves that and she may sleep.'

'I'll do that. It'll give Nanny some time to herself, too.'

He put down his cup, ruffled Lisa's hair and kissed her gently and got up. 'I'll leave you to dress, both of you, though you look very nice as you are.' He smiled slowly at her look. 'And I mustn't forget this, must I?' He bent and kissed her again, this time without haste, and Lisa laughed and clapped her hands and gabbled something to her father.

'We are agreed, Lisa and I,' he told Fran, 'that you are a perfect mama.'

'That is at least something,' said Fran tartly, and, at his sudden cold stare, instantly regretted the remark.

Despite her outward serenity, she had been nervous about her new life, but she need not have been. Nanny and Nel and Tuggs nudged her carefully through the day, always appearing just when she was in doubt about something, gently suggested coffee, a walk in the grounds with Lisa, lunch with the little girl and Nanny on the shady veranda at the back of the house, and perhaps a swim in the pool, tucked away in a corner of the gardens, while the little girl had her afternoon nap.

When Lisa awoke, she took the little girl down to the lake on the other side of the lane running past the house. By the time Litrik got home she was feeling her feet sufficiently to greet him in what she hoped was a properly wifely fashion under Lisa's sharp eyes. The three of them played cards until Lisa was borne off to bed and Litrik went to his study, saying that they would see each other at dinner. Which left Fran free to go to her room and put on one of her new dresses.

She was agreeably surprised how pleasant the evening was. True, as soon as dinner was over, Litrik excused himself once more, but they had talked easily enough over the meal and he had observed that they might expect a good many friends to call within the next few weeks and, as well as that, dinner invitations. 'And I shall be free on Saturday—we might take Lisa to the sea for the day; this weather can't last much longer and it may be our last chance.'

They had had their coffee at the table and presently Fran said, 'Well, don't let me keep you from your work,' and got to her feet, followed with unflattering briskness by Litrik. 'I'm quite tired,' she told him mendaciously, and, since Tuggs was in the room, 'don't be late, will you?'

'I'll be as quick as I can, darling.' Uttered in just the right kind of voice. She blushed and Tuggs looked sentimental.

It was too early to go to bed; she went through the hall and into the drawing room. There was a grand piano at one end with a wall sconce shining invitingly on to its keyboard. The room was only dimly lighted but there was a log fire burning in the great hearth. Fran closed the door after her, went to the piano and sat down before it. She was by no means a brilliant pianist but she had talent and feeling. Perhaps if she played for a little while she might be able to throw off the vague feeling of disquiet... Half an hour of Delius, Chopin, Debussy and as much as she could remember of the score of *Cats* soothed her, uplifting her spirits sufficiently for her to embark on *Me and My Girl* when something made her pause and look round. At the other end of the room, sitting in the great wing chair by the fire, was Litrik, stretched out comfortably in the fire's warmth.

'Don't stop,' he begged her, but she got up, closed the piano and stood very straight beside it. 'If I disturbed you, I'm sorry,' she began.

'Not in the least, you play delightfully. Did you know that Lisa loves music? You must play for her some time.'

He got up from his chair and walked towards her. 'You did not find the day too difficult?'

'No, everyone has been so kind, I—I felt quite at home.'

'Good. One day soon we must go to Utrecht and you can buy some clothes.'

'There's no need.' The idea of spending his money bothered her.

'You are mistaken. We shall be invited out; I have a number of friends who will ask us to dine and later we must give a dinner party ourselves. For these you must be suitably dressed. I am a wealthy man and well known.'

She thought of her carefully chosen wardrobe which had seemed so right when she had bought it.

Evidently it hadn't been suitable at all; he might even be ashamed of her. She swallowed mounting rage.

She said in a high voice, 'Ah—fringe benefits, how delightful. May I spend as much as I like?'

'Within reason…'

'Well, since I have no idea of your income, nor do I wish to know, that's going to be difficult, isn't it?' Her eyes glittered with temper. 'But don't worry, I'll do you proud—I've always wanted to wear *haute couture*.'

She went past him towards the door. 'You can always mortgage the house,' she told him flippantly as she closed the door behind her.

She didn't hear his low laugh; she was shaking with rage as she went up to her bed. Presently, sitting up in bed, she made a list on the back of an envelope. It was a long list; every single garment she could think of was on it and even roughly priced. The total cost ran into four figures. She cast paper and pen from her and turned out the light. She had married him to make Lisa's short life happy and for no other reason. He had said nothing about dinner parties and social occasions; well, if he wanted a dressed-up puppet he should have one. Pure silk, she reflected sleepily, cashmere, Gucci shoes and handbags and wildly expensive leather belts, she would have them all.

He played his part very nicely in the morning, joking with Lisa while they had their tea and Fran, because she had a promise to keep, was everything that Lisa expected of her. They spent another leisurely day, culminating in Litrik's return, tea on the veranda and a boisterous game of Ludo. In the evening, as the two of them sat down to dinner, he had an urgent call to go to the hospital in Utrecht, so that Fran ate alone and, since he didn't return, went to bed.

The days were falling into a pattern. It seemed that, for the time being at least, no one expected her to take over the housekeeping, something she hadn't wanted to do anyway. She was kept busy enough with Lisa, arranging the flowers, talking with Litrik's family on the telephone and, when there was a spare half hour, inspecting the cupboards Nel opened for her to look through. But as Tuggs was careful to explain, Lisa came first, the running of the house could come later.

The fine weather held; with an excited little girl cocooned on the back seat, they set out for Noordwijk-aan-zee with the dogs and a picnic hamper and somehow, once they were there, with Litrik pushing the chair along the water's edge and Fran strolling along picking up shells and seaweed for Lisa to see, she dropped her guard, laughing and talking with a surprisingly friendly Litrik, a happy state of affairs which lasted all day. It wasn't until Lisa was safely tucked up in bed and they were sitting over their drinks before dinner that Litrik leaned across and tossed a cheque book into her lap.

'Lisa is due for a check up next week—on Monday morning. I suggest that you come in with us and go shopping while she is at the hospital.'

She stared down at the cheque book. 'Perhaps Lisa would like to come with me...'

'Far too tiring. Buy all you want and bring it home to show her.'

'All I want? You mean that, Litrik?'

'Did I not say so? Indulge yourself, Francesca. Presumably you like clothes as much as any other woman?'

She thought of her carefully made out list. 'Indeed I do. It will probably need more than one morning to buy all the things that I should like.'

'You can drive. There is a Mini in the garage— you can leave Lisa with Nanny.'

She said serenely. 'Thank you, I'll do that. And may I take Lisa for short drives around the country?'

'Why not?' He sounded faintly bored. 'The roads are quiet and you say you can drive.'

Tuggs came to tell them that dinner was ready and Fran was careful to keep their talk on safe grounds. The pleasant *bonhomie* they had enjoyed on the beach had gone; she supposed that it was all part and parcel of keeping Lisa happy—when she wasn't with them there was no need to pretend. Litrik was a reserved man and Tuggs and Nel wouldn't expect him to be otherwise, even though he was so recently married. She agreed pleasantly with him about the pleasure of their day; agreed, too, that they should accept the several invitations which they had received to dine with his friends. She accompanied him to the drawing room and poured their coffee, smilingly agreed, for

Tuggs's benefit, that it was a pity that he had a lecture to prepare for his next teaching round, and picked up the knitting she had so fortunately packed, a soothing occupation, sorely needed. Her serene exterior masked a smouldering rage; Litrik had tossed the cheque book at her with the casual air of a man throwing his dog a biscuit. It had taken all her self-control not to throw it back at him, and now she was glad that she hadn't. She would go shopping and she would make sure that he wouldn't forget it in a hurry. Fran, usually so mild-tempered and kind, seethed with temper.

The knitting wasn't helping much. She went to the piano and lifted the lid and then went back to the big double door and made sure that it was closed before settling down on the piano stool. Litrik's study was on the other side of the hall and the house was large; if she kept her foot on the soft pedal, he wouldn't hear a note. She played Mendelssohn, Debussy and Grieg and at length closed the piano. She was crossing the room to pick up her knitting when a faint sound made her turn her head. Litrik was sitting in one of the big winged chairs in the bay window.

'Delightful,' he observed, 'but why the soft pedal?'

'How did you get in here?'

'Er—there is a small door from the back of the hall. I didn't want to disturb you. Even with the soft pedal down, it was obvious to me that you were taking your feelings out on the piano.'

Words—whole sentences of a vitriolic nature—

were on her tongue. She swallowed the lot, wished him an icy good night and went out of the room.

Since the next day was Sunday, they went to church, sitting in the family pew under the pulpit with Lisa in her chair between them. Fran, listening with half an ear to Dominee Meertens thundering what sounded like warnings of eternal damnation, allowed her thoughts to wander. Nothing could have been pleasanter than Litrik's manner that morning and she perforce, with Lisa's eyes upon them both, had to match his manner with her own. The strain of being a supposedly loving wife was beginning to tell on her. Being a mother to Lisa wasn't hard at all; the child responded to love like a flower to sunshine and Fran had not found it hard to love her. So unlike her father: no feelings at all, rude, arrogant and too much money for his own good. He needed taking down a peg; she would enjoy doing that. She frowned; she had entered into her pact with Litrik meaning to do all she could to help him make Lisa happy, but somehow it wasn't turning out like that at all. She was allowing her personal feelings to take over and it was Lisa who mattered. She glanced down at the little face beside hers and smiled and tucked a small hand in hers, promising herself silently that she would keep a guard on her tongue and try harder to like Litrik. She would, she reflected, like him very much if only he were different. She was prevented from pursuing this line of thought by Dominee Meerten's rolling periods coming to a stop and everyone getting to their feet for prayers.

Presently they made their way down the aisle to shake the *dominee*'s hand and then chat with acquaintances of Litrik. It was a splendid opportunity for Fran to air her sparse Dutch, which she did reluctantly but with an unconscious charm which earned her a good deal of praise, even if it was unmerited. What with that and her good resolutions during the sermon, the day proved to be pleasant enough. Litrik laid himself out to be an amusing companion and Lisa was at her happiest; it wasn't hard for Fran to play her part.

Indeed the day had gone so well that before she went to sleep she had almost decided to tear up her shopping list and make out another one of three or four basic outfits, reasonably priced. It was unfortunate that when she went down to breakfast, dressed for the day in one of the jersey outfits, Litrik should look up from his letters to remark, 'Ah, Mama Mouse, shortly to be turned into a swan, if I may mix my metaphors.' His cool gaze took in her unassuming appearance. 'And very much the mouse.'

Tuggs wasn't in the room and Lisa for some reason hadn't yet joined them. Fran sat down and poured herself some coffee with a hand which shook slightly and helped herself to a croissant.

'What—nothing to say?' His voice was silky; he was needling her.

She buttered her croissant and took some black cherry jam. She had no idea why he was being so nasty but she didn't intend to let him see how much it could upset her. Mentally she added a few items unnecessary and expensive, to her shopping list. She had her rage nicely under control by now; she said serenely, 'I expect you've had a bad night, you'll feel better when you've had your breakfast. Sleeplessness always makes one scratchy…'

She gave him a clear look and a kindly smile as she spoke and was rewarded by his look of affront. And then disconcerted by his bellow of laughter. Nanny came in then with Lisa who wanted to know why he was laughing and he became gentle at once, giving her some joking explanation which made her laugh, too.

At the end of the meal Litrik said, 'You'll come to the hospital with us, Francesca; you can say goodbye to Lisa there—the shops are close by. The car will be in the hospital forecourt but if you want to leave parcels let the porter have them. We shan't be ready until noon at the earliest.'

She agreed calmly and with a smile, careful to preserve her image for Lisa's benefit, and the two of them went off to get ready for their trip to Utrecht, happily engrossed in the peculiar mixture of English and Dutch which they had made their own.

The hospital was vast and impressive; Fran would have liked to have seen more of it, but once they were inside Litrik had suggested, in the pleasant voice he used when Lisa was with them, that she should say goodbye for the present. So she said, *'Tot ziens,'* in a cheerful voice, hugged the little girl, smiled at Litrik and took herself off. It was barely nine o'clock. She had three hours and some of that time must be taken up with spying out the land. She nipped smartly into the centre of the city, only a few minutes' walk from the hospital, and did a rapid survey of the shops. There were plenty to choose from and at the end of half an hour she had earmarked the boutiques which had taken her fancy. By eleven o'clock she was able to heave a contented sigh and pause for coffee. Sitting at a pavement café outside a fashionable department store, she conned her list. She was, to date, the possessor of two of the new season's suits, one in a rich bronze tweed, the other in a soft blue wool, a beautifully cut and frightfully expensive winter coat, a couple of gaily patterned knitted outfits, a dark green suede skirt and waistcoat with silk—pure silk— blouses to wear with them, three after-six dresses in strikingly rich colours and several pairs of shoes, high-heeled and impractical; it seemed only sense to have bought a pair of soft leather boots as well. She found time to buy undies, too, and a quilted satin dressing-gown and matching slippers. It only remained to go then to the particular boutique she had earmarked and see if she could find suitable evening dresses. Never mind if she didn't have the chance to wear them; Litrik had told her to buy all she wanted: and she very much wanted the peach pink organza dress she had seen in the window.

She had less than an hour and she would have to

collect several of the dress boxes she had arranged to pick up at the end of the morning. Much refreshed by the coffee she set off briskly.

The pink organza was even lovelier on than it was in the window. She hardly recognised herself when she tried it on for it fitted to perfection. Heaven send she would have an opportunity to wear it… The sales lady was middle-aged and clever and she spoke English.

'We have some charming dresses if Mevrouw would care to look at them?' She suggested, 'If Mevrouw leads a social life now is the time to choose a gown of the first fashion.'

'Something for dinner parties.' Fran already had her eye on a deep apricot crêpe dress with long sleeves and a pretty neckline. 'And I believe we have to go the *burgermeester*'s reception…'

'Mevrouw's husband is well known in Utrecht?'

'He is a doctor. Dr van Rijgen…'

The lady's eyes gleamed. 'Ah, yes, a distinguished man indeed. The wedding was reported in the paper recently. My felicitations, Mevrouw. And may I suggest the apricot crêpe and perhaps this Prussian blue silk with the pleated skirt—just the thing for a dinner party.'

Fran bought them all, paid their astronomical cost without batting an eyelid and, since she was assured that the dresses would be packed and sent immediately to the hospital, set off to collect the rest of her shopping.

She had to make two journeys and, slightly alarmed at the pile of dress boxes the porter obligingly stacked in his office, she waited. He had barely finished when she saw a nurse wheeling Lisa into the entrance hall and went to meet her.

Lisa hugged her as though she had been gone for days instead of hours, and Fran knelt down beside the chair and put her arms round the thin little body. 'You were a really good girl?' she asked, and repeated it in her fragmentary Dutch so that Lisa shrilled with giggles.

'You were missed,' said Litrik from behind her. 'Next time you must come, too.'

Fran got to her feet. 'I would have come this morning, but I wasn't asked.' She spoke lightly because probably the nurse could understand English and Lisa was watching them both.

'She's been a good girl she tells me.'

'Very good. We must think of a little treat for her. You have done your shopping?'

She looked so pleased with herself that he studied her face thoughtfully.

'Yes, thank you. My parcels are in the porter's lodge.'

The doctor watched everything being loaded into the car boot with an expressionless face. Fran, busy getting Lisa comfortable, glanced at him once and decided that he was furiously angry, but when he got into the car and turned to look at her she was surprised to see that he was smiling, his eyes gleaming with amusement.

'Paid in my own coin,' he murmured. 'For a mouse you pack a hefty punch, Francesca.'

And before she could reply he said something to Lisa which sent her off into peals of laughter. 'I can see that there will be no need to amuse Lisa for the rest of the day; she will want to see the lot and, from the look of things, that's going to take hours.'

Fran thought it prudent not to answer that but let Lisa chatter for the short drive back home. She had indeed paid him back in his own coin but strangely she didn't feel happy about it.

CHAPTER SIX

THEY had lunch as soon as they got in for Litrik had to go to his consulting rooms in the afternoon and then on to the hospital at Zeist.

The boxes and parcels had been borne upstairs and Fran, eyeing their number, went down to lunch feeling guilty. But Litrik made no mention of her morning, the talk was light-hearted while Fran coaxed the little girl, now very tired, to eat something, and presently when the meal was finished she said, 'I'll take her up to her bed—shall I keep her there for tea?'

'A very good idea. Why don't you take your shopping to the nursery when she wakes up and keep her amused while she rests? She can get up for her supper if she wants to; I'll leave that to you—I'll not be back until late this evening.'

Nanny was waiting; Fran told her what Litrik had advised and then went downstairs again. He was in the hall on the point of leaving.

'Before you go, how is she?'

He had his hand on the door and turned to look at her. 'Not good, I'm afraid.' His voice held no expression. 'We must make the best of September and October.'

'Litrik, I'm so very sorry.' Her heart was wrung

with pity; without stopping to think she ran across the few yards between them and put her hand over his.

He didn't say anything but he looked down at her hand clasping his, his eyebrows lifted and she snatched away her hand as though his had been red hot. If he had slapped her face she couldn't have been more shocked.

He opened the door then and went out without a backward glance, leaving her standing there, near to tears. When the sound of the car had died away she went into the drawing room and out into the garden through the doors at its end. The weather was still delightful but now there was a hint of early autumn in the air but her shiver had nothing to do with the cool wind. He was a monster, she told herself, and knew that that wasn't true. A monster couldn't love a child as he loved Lisa; go to such lengths to keep her happy. She went and sat under the mulberry tree until Tuggs came to find her. 'Mevrouw van Rijgen wishes to speak to you on the telephone, Mevrouw, if you would take the call in the drawing room?'

A dinner party, suggested Litrik's mother, quite an informal one, if they could manage the following Saturday evening. 'Just a few friends,' said Mevrouw van Rijgen kindly. 'I want to show you off, my dear!'

'It sounds delightful, but I'll have to ask Litrik. May I phone you back in the morning? He is not at home at present and I don't expect him back until later this evening.'

'Of course, my dear. How is Lisa?' And, when

Fran hesitated, 'Things aren't so good, are they? I won't bother you with questions now. Ring me tomorrow, Francesca.'

Tuggs had put tea in the small sitting room, fussing gently around her, saying as he left her, 'We're all that upset to hear that Lisa isn't so well, Mevrouw. The doctor'll be cut to the heart and you, too—she loves you like you were her real mother.'

'Oh, Tuggs, I do hope so, but I've known her such a short time. You must all feel very bad about it. I—feel an interloper…'

He was quite shocked. 'Indeed no, Mevrouw. We're thankful that the doctor found you in time.'

'Thank you, Tuggs.' She remembered something. 'The doctor says that I may drive the Mini in the garage. I thought I'd take Lisa out sometimes—not far, but the country is so pretty and perhaps we can stop for tea or just to admire the view.'

'She'll like that. I'll see that the Mini is ready for you whenever you want it, Mevrouw.'

She smiled at his kind face. 'Thank you, Tuggs. You—all of you—have been so good to me.'

'A pleasure, Mevrouw. Will you be going to sit with Lisa this evening?'

'Yes. When I've had tea I'll spend the evening with her. The doctor will be back late this evening—you know that already?'

When he had gone she drank her tea and ate one or two of the little biscuits Nel had made and then presently went up to the nursery. Lisa was still sleeping but as Fran went in soft-footed, nodding to Nanny, knitting at the table, the little girl awoke.

'Tea,' she demanded, and to Fran, 'Mama stay.'

'Nanny, could you ask Nel to let us have a tray of tea? I've just had mine but Lisa might eat something if we have it together.'

And as Nanny got to her feet. 'I'm going to show the things I bought today to Lisa so we'll be all right until it's her bed time. Should we get her up for an hour or two do you think?'

'In her dressing-gown perhaps, Mevrouw. You will be all right?'

Fran nodded. 'Oh yes, Nanny. You go and have your tea in peace.'

Tea came and they shared the small meal together, and then Fran went to her room and fetched the pile of dress boxes.

She dressed in one outfit after the other with Lisa sitting in her chair clapping her hands and laughing with delight. The evening dresses were left until the last and by that time it was Lisa's time for supper and bed. Nanny, coming back, stopped in the doorway to exclaim, 'Mevrouw, what a beautiful dress—you look so pretty!'

Her warm admiration made Fran glow with pleasure; the pink was indeed beautiful and even in her over-critical eyes she looked less mousy in it. She said almost shyly, 'There's the *burgermeester*'s reception in a few weeks, would it do for that?'

The three of them spent a happy half hour examining everything and then Fran got out of the pink dress and into her sober jersey and, while Nanny saw to Lisa, took everything back to her room and hung each garment lovingly in the clothes closet. Tomorrow she would wear one of the knitted outfits, the saffron coloured skirt and patterned jerkin and one of those silk blouses. She sat down for a moment and took out her list. She had noted the prices of everything on it, now she added them up. The total made her gasp; even if Litrik were very rich, he would surely have something to say about the astronomical amount she had written down.

They played their part in the morning, with Lisa tucked up in Fran's bed with an affable Litrik sitting at its foot, drinking his tea. Fran scanned his face and marvelled that he was the same man as the coldly angry one of yesterday evening. Probably, she thought wryly, he'll look like that again when he sees how much I've spent.

She made an excuse to go down to breakfast before Lisa was dressed and found Litrik already there. He got up when she went into the room and she admired—for the hundredth time—his easy good manners.

She went straight to him and laid her neat list beside his plate.

'That's what I spent yesterday.' Try as she might her voice shook a little.

He waited until she was sitting down, pouring coffee with an unsteady hand, before he picked it up and read it. If she had expected anger or surprise she was to be disappointed. His face remained blandly calm and he showed no surprise. She said uncertainly, 'It's rather a lot of money…'

'I believe that I told you to buy what you wanted,' he observed, his voice as bland as his face. Without a trace of sarcasm he went on, 'Perhaps you didn't have sufficient time yesterday; if you need another few hours in Utrecht you can come in with me after lunch—I shall be home by noon—I'll be at my consulting rooms until four o'clock.'

She studied his face; it showed nothing but a disinterested politeness.

'I shan't need any more clothes for months,' she told him and saw the look of disbelief on his face. 'Besides, I've promised Lisa that we'll go for a short drive this afternoon—I'll be very careful.'

'Of course! We dine at Uncle Hilwert's on Friday, do we not? Not too many of us, I believe, and it won't be black ties.' He picked up the first of his letters. 'You'll forgive me if I read my post? There's not much chance once Lisa is here.'

So she drank some coffee and ate some toast, small and mouselike and unassuming despite the saffron skirt and the gaily coloured jerkin. For all the doctor cared, she might have been wearing an old sack; he hadn't even noticed… But Lisa did; she was examined, exclaimed over and admired by the little girl while Litrik smiled at her chatter and said nothing. Presently he got up to go, kissed his small daughter, and then paused by Fran's chair to brush her cheek lightly. 'I like the outfit—a great improvement,' he murmured.

He came home for lunch as he had promised but he had no time to linger over the meal. Nanny whisked Lisa away for her rest and Fran went in search of Tuggs to get a road map from him. The Veluwe would be too far, she had decided, but there was a good sweep of pleasantly wooded country and heath all around them. She pored over the country roads within a radius of twenty miles or so and planned their trip, avoiding the towns, criss-crossing the woods; the roads would be narrow but she was a good driver and there wouldn't be much traffic.

Under Tuggs's fatherly eye they set off presently, going eastwards from Ziest, taking a country road which would take her eventually in the direction of Doorn. She didn't intend to enter the small town, but by-pass it and drive on towards Maarn, turning north, making a rough circle. They had passed Maarn, gone under the motorway and taken a road between thick woods when they reached a crossroad. Fran had planned to go straight ahead, but Lisa had other ideas. The road to the left was nothing more than a narrow brick lane, overhung with trees, the signpost offering no more than four kilometres to Emminheide; not even marked on the map, when Fran looked for it. But nothing she could say would persuade Lisa to change her mind. She wanted to go to Emminheide and Fran gave in.

The road, being brick and rural, was uneven and only wide enough for one car. She drove slowly, since the road, unlike most Dutch roads, wound itself round a multitude of corners and the trees on either side prevented her from seeing any distance ahead. The woods on either side became, if anything, even thicker and she felt decided relief when they passed a small cottage, set back from the road. And presently they reached Emminheide: a cluster of small houses, a very large church and that was all. Fran drove on, wondering where the road led, for it must end somewhere, and after another half mile or so they saw another cottage, standing by itself in a small clearing; trees all around it, a well-tended little garden between it and the lane. There was an old woman in the garden and when she saw them she stopped picking the plums from a tree by the cottage and came down to the gate. Fran stopped and called good day and the old woman answered cheerfully.

'Tea?' asked Lisa.

There was no harm in asking. Fran drove the car carefully up to the gate and began a careful request for a drink for Lisa. She added politely in her best Dutch, 'I will pay you, Mevrouw.'

The old woman came out of the gate and peered into the car, and she and Lisa carried out a brief conversation, at the end of which she turned to Fran. She spoke slowly now—Lisa must have told her that Fran's Dutch was fragmentary. Of course they could have tea. If Mevrouw would like to carry the poor little girl into the cottage they might sit in comfort and when they were rested, before they returned, they might like to see the lake behind the cottage. So beautiful, added the old woman, and very few people know of it.

There was plenty of time; Fran carried Lisa into the cottage and sat her down in the tiny parlour, seldom used except for important occasions such as weddings or funerals or family visits. It was overfull of tables and chairs and the walls were hung with old-fashioned pictures and photos, but there were some pieces of beautiful old china and a little cabinet housed silver spoons and dishes. They sat at the round table in the centre of the room and drank their tea and ate wafer thin biscuits, and when they had finished, Fran paid their modest bill and asked if they might see the lake. 'If it's not too far—I have to carry the little girl.'

The old woman nodded and smiled and led the way to the side of the garden and pointed to a path through the trees. Fran couldn't understand what she was saying but Lisa did and the child nodded and said, 'Two minutes, Mama.'

'You are learning English far quicker than I am learning Dutch,' said Fran, and laughed and at the same time sighed inwardly for Lisa's light weight seemed even lighter each time she picked her up.

The path was easy and well defined, leading through closely planted trees with no hint of what was to come. It ended abruptly at the edge of a fairytale pond, not large, but ringed with trees, fringed with rushes and reeds, its water a clear green dappled by sunshine. There were water coots among the reeds and the plop of fish. There was a willow tree drooping into the water and in season, Fran guessed, there would be kingcups, flags and meadowsweet. From where she stood she could see a water vole motionless on the bank. She heard Lisa's happy sigh and the skinny arms tightened round her neck. 'Pretty,' said Lisa. 'Stay.'

'All right, darling, just for a few minutes.' Fran walked carefully round the pond until she came to a fallen tree stump and then she sat down. 'Story,' demanded Lisa and, after a moment's thought, 'fairies.'

So Fran started off on one of her rather vague fairytales, made up as she went along, half Dutch and half English. But Lisa didn't seem to mind that, she listened avidly to every word, nodding her small head from time to time and, when Fran paused for breath, urging her on again.

'Look,' said Fran at last, 'I'll ask the old woman if we can come here some afternoons and have tea and sit here…'

She tried again in Dutch and Lisa understood. *'Geheim,'* she said, so seriously that Fran did her best to understand her, but in the end she said apologetically, 'Sorry, darling, I don't understand.'

Lisa pondered. *'Niemand,'* she ventured. Fran knew that. 'No one.'

'Weet,' said Lisa hopefully.

'Know?' cried Fran truly triumphantly. 'You clever girl! Secret, of course.'

They hugged each other for being so clever and then Fran carried her back down the path to the car and settled her in it before going to speak to the old woman who had come to the door to watch them. It took a little time to explain and in the end Lisa did it for her. The old woman nodded, pleased to have visitors and to earn a few *gulden* and after a deal of hand shaking, Fran turned the car and drove back the way they had come. They had stayed longer than she had meant to and even if Litrik wasn't home, Nel and Tuggs would worry.

They had time to tidy themselves up before he arrived and when he asked if they had had a pleasant drive Lisa burst into speech. He listened patiently and then said to Fran, 'I gather you've had an exciting afternoon, all very secret?'

'We had a lovely time,' said Fran, 'and yes, it's secret but quite harmless. I promised I wouldn't tell...' She hesitated. 'You don't mind?'

'Mind, my dear girl? Lisa has never been so happy. Far from minding I am deeply in your debt.'

He went over to little Lisa, sitting happy in her chair. 'What is it to be this evening?' he asked Fran over his shoulder. 'Snakes and Ladders or Ludo?'

He picked up the child and went to sit down in the big chair by the table and repeated everything in Dutch. It was to be Snakes and Ladders; Fran got the board and the counters and presently the three of them were deep in the game, cheating from time to time so that Lisa should win.

As Friday drew near, Fran found that she was nervous. She liked Oom Hilwert though he was a bit outspoken, but supposing there were people there she didn't know? Who couldn't speak English? Litrik would be ashamed of her... Common sense came to her rescue; everyone knew that her Dutch was of the kindergarten variety. She would wear one of her lovely new dresses and do her hair in the french pleat she had been experimenting with for the last day or two in the privacy of her bedroom. And if he didn't like it he could lump it, she told herself vigorously.

She took Lisa to the secret pool on Friday and they sat in the afternoon sunshine while she continued her fairytale, and then she carried Lisa to the cottage where the old woman gave them tea. And when they got home, since Litrik hadn't returned, Fran took the little girl up to her room and showed her the dress that she was going to wear that evening.

Litrik was late home; Lisa was already in bed by the time he got in and there was barely an hour before they had to leave for Oom Hilwert's house. They went together, as they always did, to say good night to her and after a whispered promise that she would come back, dressed for the evening, Fran left the two of them together.

The dress was beautiful. Fran, who had never had couture clothes and had always thought of them as being wildly expensive, suitable only for the models in *Vogue,* realised that she had been wrong. The dress transformed her; it clung where it should, fell free in graceful folds when she walked, and made her feel like royalty. She had managed the french pleat, too, and put on a pair of high-heeled satin slippers which added both to her height and her self-esteem. She picked up her little beaded bag, which she had been unable to resist, and the soft angora stole and went along to Lisa's nursery. The child was still awake and Fran sat down on the side of the bed and showed her the contents of her bag, allowed her to sniff the fine white hanky scented with *L'air du temps,* and then pirouetted slowly so that the full glories of the dress might be studied.

'Darling Mama,' said Lisa sleepily as Fran kissed her good night.

Downstairs Litrik was waiting, immaculate in a dark grey suit and a richly sober tie. She had expected, or at least hoped, that he would say something about her dress, even tell her that she looked nice, but although he studied her through half-closed lids for several seconds, all he said was, 'I should like you to wear these,' and handed her a long velvet box.

There was a double row of pearls inside with a diamond clasp. She took it out with delicate fingers and looked at him, and when he didn't speak said quietly, 'The family expect it, of course...'

He nodded. 'Yes, they've been in the family for a very long time—they're handed down.'

'Or lent,' said Fran matter-of-factly as she fastened

the clasp and went to take a look in the great carved mirror over the fireplace. They were magnificent and she touched them lightly while a dim memory became sharp in her head. 'Pearls around the neck, stones upon the heart': a proverb dredged up from something she must have read a long time ago. And oh, so true. She turned away from the mirror. 'Must I wear them?'

'Of course.' He sounded a little impatient. 'You are my wife.'

She stood in front of him, her head a little on one side, looking at him. 'No, I'm not,' she corrected him. 'I'm Lisa's Mama. We mustn't let the whole thing get out of hand, must we?' There was faint rebuke in her quiet voice. She gave him a kindly smile. 'It's difficult, isn't it? It seemed simple enough. Besides, I hate deceiving people, don't you?'

He said very evenly, 'I believe I made it perfectly clear that I will do anything to make Lisa happy for the next few weeks—we can go into the rights and wrongs of the matter at the appropriate time.' He turned away. 'If you are ready, shall we go?'

They hardly spoke in the car and when they got to Oom Hilwert's house there was no need to for they were at once surrounded by the other guests. Fran had to admire Litrik's manner towards her, though: the considerate husband, steering her from one guest to the other, making sure that she had the drink she wanted, bringing her into the conversation, encouraging her to take part in it, so that before they went into dinner she was quite at her ease. She sat on Oom Hilwert's right, with a youngish man, a distant cousin of the family, on her other side, and between them they flattered her gently, admiring her dress, remarking on the pearls, and reiterating their pleasure in having her in the family. 'And I daresay Litrik's loaded you with jewellery,' observed Oom Hilwert, 'though you have the good sense not to wear anything but pearls with that dress.'

'Litrik wanted me to wear them,' said Fran serenely. It was a pity that he was sitting at the other end of the table and couldn't hear.

After dinner everyone gathered once more in the drawing room, a vast apartment heavily furnished and rather grand and gloomy. The talk was largely of the *burgermeester*'s reception on one evening the following week and led to the ladies gathering together to discuss what they intended wearing.

'And you, my dear?' enquired Litrik's mother. 'You have a pretty dress, no doubt. You look charming this evening.'

Fran thanked her nicely. 'Well I found a dress in Utrecht—it's pink...'

'Just the right colour for you, Francesca. You will be able to wear the earrings.'

Fran said warily, 'Oh, yes...' and was saved from saying more by Litrik strolling over to join them.

'Francesca, Oom Hilwert would like you to play for us.'

She smiled up at him while her eyes flashed indignant fire. There was no point in making a fuss and she wasn't going to give him the satisfaction of knowing that he had spoilt her evening. She crossed the room to the grand piano standing in one corner and sat herself down, outwardly composed.

'What would you like me to play?' she asked Oom Hilwert. 'I'm not used to playing in front of people and I'm only a tolerable player.'

The old gentleman beamed at her. 'Play what you wish, my dear, and we will enjoy it.'

She ran her capable little hands over the keys; it was a splendid instrument and she would try and do it justice. She began with Delius and then Schubert and wandered on through Frans Lehar and Strauss and Grieg and then back to Delius, stopping as quietly as she had begun, sitting with her hands in her lap.

They had sat quietly while she played, now they clapped and crowded round her, making much of her and someone said, 'Lucky Litrik, to come home to that in the evenings,' and everyone laughed and someone else said, 'I'll settle for Francesca, never mind the piano,' and they all laughed again. Fran laughed with them, taking care not to look at Litrik.

Driving home presently he said blandly, 'You were a great success, Francesca.' They were driving fast down the almost empty motorway. 'You didn't mind my making you play?'

She was astonished to discover that she wanted to cry. She said stonily. 'I minded very much, it was a rotten trick.' She added childishly, 'It would have served you right if I had sat down at the piano and played chopsticks.'

'Yes, it would, wouldn't it?' he agreed affably, 'only I knew that you wouldn't do that. Do you want me to apologise?' His voice was silky.

'Certainly not. It's of no consequence to me. After all you are behaving as I would expect you to behave.'

'Now why do you say that?' He sounded interested and amused, too.

'Anyone—any man who can reduce student nurses to a mass of shaking nerves before a lecture hall of people, is capable of any mean trick he chooses to think up.'

All he said was, 'For a mouse you have sharp teeth.'

She would have liked to have gone straight to her room when they got home but she stood in the hall, waiting for him while he took the car round to the garages at the side of the house. He looked at her and smiled as he came in and locked the door behind him. 'Friends again?' he wanted to know, and she heard the mocking note in his voice.

'No. Here are your pearls. Thank you for lending them to me.' She was of half a mind to tell him what his mother had said about the earrings. Let him find out for himself, she decided and uttered a rather gruff good night as she went up the staircase.

Litrik was free on the following day; they drove to the Veluwe and had a picnic under the trees, Lisa in a woolly jacket and Fran in the suede outfit, for there was a distinct nip in the air. Litrik was at his most urbane and Lisa was as merry as a cricket. Fran, watching her, couldn't believe that she was going to die. Watching Litrik, too, laughing and joking with her as though he hadn't a care in the world, she stifled a sudden deep sympathy for him. He had, after all, known of the situation for months and must have become reconciled to it. He looked up and caught her watching him and for a moment they stared at each other and then he turned away to tease Lisa gently and presently they were all engrossed in Lisa's favourite occupation—teaching Fran Dutch.

Almost a week went by, each day with its gentle routine and two more visits to the fairy pond where they sat, the two of them, while Fran laboriously wove her fairytale, almost as absorbed in it as her small listener. The old woman seemed to enjoy them coming, too; their tea was laid out for them in her little parlour and she liked a chat before they went home, sometimes leaving it to the last minute so that they were barely indoors and sitting in the drawing room before Litrik came back. For that was part of the secret; when he enquired as to their afternoon, Lisa would say that they had had a nice drive in the car and exchange a smile with Fran. 'Nice, Mama?' she would ask and Fran would answer, *'Geweldig,'* just to let Litrik see that she was learning Dutch fast.

They didn't go to the pond on the afternoon of the *burgermeester*'s reception; getting dressed for it

would take up most of the evening and Lisa was to
have a ringside seat from Fran's bed. As it turned out
Litrik phoned to say that he would be home later than
usual and they weren't to wait for him to have tea,
so that the two of them, with Nanny for company,
went up to Fran's room where she laid out the pink
dress and, leaving Lisa in Nanny's company, went to
take a bath. She had washed her hair the evening before and it hung very clean and shining around her
shoulders—they wasted a good deal of time arranging
it in various styles before she sat down in front of her
dressing-table and did her face, applying the expensive new make-up she had bought. It didn't seem to
make much difference and she turned her attention to
her hair, putting it up in its usual french pleat, wishing
the while that it was a dramatic black or dazzling
blonde. It was time to put on the dress and she stood
before the pier-glass studying her image while Lisa
and Nanny uttered little cries of admiration. Well, the
face and the hair might not be anything to shout
about, but the dress certainly was. She danced a few
steps round the room for Lisa's pleasure and stopped
when there was a knock at the door and Litrik came
in, dressed save for his tailcoat.

He dropped a kiss on Fran's cheek, hugged Lisa
and wished Nanny a good evening and then sat down
on the bed, his arm round the little girl, and studied
Fran. Lisa babbled excitedly and he said, 'Very nice,
very nice indeed, Mama—Lisa thinks you look like a
princess.' He got up and fished the pearls out of a

trouser pocket and, because Lisa and Nanny were watching, fastened them round her throat. 'Oh, and these,' he told her.

Pearl and diamond earrings, glittering and gleaming under the bright lights of the bedroom. She took them silently and went to put them on before the mirror and then, mindful as she was of their audience, turned to smile at him and thank him in her serene way.

'They look well enough,' he told her and went away to shrug himself into his tails, while she picked up the wide swansdown stole the saleslady had assured her was just the thing to wear with the gown. Litrik came back presently to say good night to Lisa and then stood patiently while she hugged and kissed Fran who bade Nanny good night and then rustled out of the room. She was scared stiff of the evening ahead of her. To anyone else she would have voiced her fright, but not to Litrik; instead she made rather vague small talk as he drove her into Utrecht.

She need not have worried. The *burgermeester* was a genial old man with white whiskers and twinkling blue eyes and his wife, small and round and grey-haired, was just as nice. Fran, with Litrik at her elbow, was introduced, chatted to and handed on to more dignitaries, all of whom appeared to be on the best of terms with Litrik and only too willing to get on the same terms with her. Presently there was dancing and they circled the floor rather sedately before Litrik relinquished her to one of the *wethouders,* who wanted to know if an English mayor and alderman were the same as the Dutch.

'All except for the names I think,' said Fran. 'This is a very handsome ballroom.'

She couldn't have picked a more suitable subject; she was treated to a long history of the *gemeentehuis* which lasted through the dance and a couple of encores before she was whisked away by one of Litrik's cousins, a young man, not much older than herself. 'You look beautiful,' he told her gaily and she laughed. 'It's the earrings,' she explained. 'I'm terrified of losing one, though.'

She danced without pause until supper was announced and Litrik very properly came to claim her. She thought that he looked a little severe and wondered guiltily if she should have sat out some of the dances with various of the elderly ladies. 'Shouldn't I have danced so much?' she asked anxiously, 'I rather forgot who I was...'

'I am delighted to see that you are enjoying yourself, Francesca. Certainly you may dance as much as you wish. I expect you would like to sit at a table with some of your partners.' He raised a hand to a half-filled table at the other end of the room and took her arm. There were half a dozen young men and girls there and she sat down happily while Litrik went to fetch her some food. He came back with an assortment of chicken patties, vol-au-vents and tiny sandwiches and sat down beside her. He wasn't severe any more. He seemed to be on such excellent terms with everyone there; indeed, she was vexed to see that he was deliberately charming the three girls, something he had never attempted to do with her. Deep inside her she felt sad and bewildered by it. She shook the feeling off and applied herself to the talk around her, laughing rather more than she usually did.

They danced together again after supper and for the last dance. She couldn't but help notice the sentimental glances the older ladies were casting upon them. Litrik had noticed, too; he said gravely to the top of her head, 'You do realise that I am considered to be a very lucky man?'

It was on the tip of her tongue to ask him if he considered himself lucky, too, but she refrained. Instead she said worriedly, 'Really, it would have been better if I weren't to meet so many people. I could have had a cold or something—I mean, it would be easier for later on.'

He said very quietly, 'Shall we cross that bridge when we come to it, Francesca?'

It was late when they got back home and the house was quiet. 'There will be coffee in the kitchen if you want it,' Litrik told her, but she shook her head. 'I'll go to bed. I'll take a peep at Lisa first.' She paused at the bottom of the staircase and asked in a forlorn voice, 'Did I look nice?'

She thought he wasn't going to answer her. 'Very nice,' he said at length in a dry as dust voice. He wasn't even looking at her, but brushing something off his coat sleeve. He looked very handsome standing there and quite remote. She took off the pearls and unhooked the earrings and retraced her steps and handed them to him. Her good night was uttered in her usual quiet voice although she didn't look at him. She went up the stairs carefully because her eyes were full of tears and she couldn't see very clearly.

She undressed slowly, hung up the pink dress and got into a nightie and then crept along to the nursery; Lisa was asleep and so was Nanny in her room leading off it. The little girl's face looked pale and thin in the dim light of the bedside lamp and Fran felt anxiety grip her; the child looked dreadfully ill... She gave a gasp of pure fright as a hand came down on her shoulder.

'Don't worry,' said Litrik quietly into her ear, 'she is no worse. It's just that when she's sleeping it's more obvious how ill she is.' He gave her a friendly pat. 'Go to bed, Francesca.'

She turned away. 'Yes, of course.' She gave him a brief glance and he said softly, 'Why, you've been crying.'

He bent and kissed her on her gentle mouth, not the usual peck she was offered for appearances' sake, but hard and urgent. 'Go to bed,' he said, suddenly harsh, and she went without a word.

Before she slept she decided that he had been sorry for her because she had been crying about Lisa. But she had been crying before then, although she wasn't at all sure why.

September slid slowly towards October, taking

with it a round of dinner parties, family meetings and lunches, pleasant leisurely drives through the Veluwe, and the now regular afternoon visits to the fairy pool. But it was getting too chilly to stay long by the water now. Fran, with Lisa wrapped in a rug on her lap, would sit on their favourite tree stump and add another chapter to her interminable story and then hurry back to the cottage for tea and a biscuit. And the day came when she knew that Lisa wasn't well enough to go there any more; fortunately the weather changed and they were forced to stay indoors and she continued her tale telling sitting comfortably in a high-backed chair drawn up to the log fire in the great hearth, with Lisa cuddled on her lap. She didn't need the sight of Litrik's grave face to warn her that there wasn't much longer to go now, although when he was with Lisa he presented a carefree manner and laughed and joked with her as he had always done. He said nothing to Fran, for there was no need, but she and Nanny, when there was no one about, talked about it and wept a little, something Fran thought Litrik wouldn't tolerate.

And the day came when Lisa stayed in bed and from then on Fran and Nanny took it in turns to be with her, only leaving when Litrik came home, to sit by the bed and always talk cheerfully to Lisa about his day's work and his plans for Christmas; and Lisa, lying propped up against her pillows with her mouse bride beside her, listened happily.

It wasn't long before there came a day when Litrik,

too, stayed at home, sitting by the child's bed, her hand in his, talking to her in a perfectly normal voice with Nanny sitting knitting at the table and Fran on the other side of the bed stitching dolls' clothes which would never be needed. Tuggs brought trays of coffee and sandwiches and during the afternoon Litrik told Fran and Nanny to go into the garden for half an hour, but nobody wanted meals and nobody made any attempt to undress that night. Lisa died, as they had prayed she would, in her sleep just as the sun was turning a chilly dawn into a bright morning.

CHAPTER SEVEN

THAT evening, sitting alone by the fire in the drawing room after sharing a dinner with Litrik which neither of them had eaten, Fran went back over the long sad day. She had seen very little of Litrik; he had gone to his study and telephoned the hospital and Professor van Tromp, who had been looking after Lisa, and then he had emerged to shower and shave and drink a cup of coffee before shutting himself up in his study again. His face had been a grey mask of tiredness and he had hardly spoken to her. Professor van Tromp had come shortly after breakfast and when he had left again, she had gone to the nursery to help Nanny, thankful that in that kindly young woman's company she could cry if she wanted to. Litrik hadn't come to lunch; Tuggs had taken a tray of coffee to the study and she had sat at the table, pushing the food round her plate. In the afternoon she had wandered round the garden, longing to help Litrik in some way, but when she had offered to do so that morning he had told her curtly that he would do everything necessary and would telephone the family.

Even a walk with the dogs had been denied her for in the early afternoon he had emerged, whistled to Muff and Thor and left the house with them. When he had returned she had offered tea and been curtly thanked and refused.

It would have been so much easier for them both if they could have talked about Lisa and comforted each other, but he didn't want her sympathy nor had he any to offer her. Dominee Meertens had come in the morning and spent a little time talking to her but she had been too unhappy to listen, although she had been grateful.

She looked up in surprise as the *stoelklok* chimed midnight and Tuggs came into the room. 'Shall I lock up, Mevrouw?' he wanted to know. 'The doctor is in his study and I don't like to disturb him. The dogs are with him or I'd have given them a run...'

'You lock up, Tuggs, and I'll go and see if the doctor will go to bed. He must be tired; there has been so much to do.' She smiled at him from a sad face and he smiled back.

'It's been a bad day for us all, Mevrouw. Shall Nel fetch you up a nice warm drink before you sleep?'

She shook her head. 'No, thank you, Tuggs; if Nel would leave the coffee on the hob I'll get the doctor a cup if he wants it. You and Nel go to bed. You had a wakeful night and a long day, too.'

The house was very quiet once he had made it secure for the night. Fran sat on by the dying fire, thinking about Lisa and the fun they had had together. At least the little girl had been happy and had loved her a little, just as she had loved Lisa. When next she looked at the clock it was almost an hour later and she got up and crossed the hall to the study and knocked on the door and, without waiting for an answer, went in.

Litrik was sitting at his desk sprawled in his chair, staring ahead of him, his face a calm mask. He glanced at her briefly. 'What do you want, Francesca?'

'Litrik, come to bed, it's gone one o'clock and you had no sleep last night.' And when he took no notice, she went up close to him and said gently, 'Lisa was so happy and content, can you not try and think of that? And she loved you and you loved her as you always will. I—I'm so sorry, Litrik...'

He said with a kind of cold politeness, 'What can you possibly know about it? You haven't had a child!'

She didn't answer that. 'Would you like some coffee? Nel left it ready.'

'No, thank you. Go away, Francesca. Just for a time you and I have nothing to say to each other.'

He was wrong, of course, but she saw that she wouldn't be able to make him see that. Feeling defeated, she left him there alone.

He was at the breakfast table in the morning and wished her good morning and expressed the hope that she had slept well. 'I shall be at home today,' he told her. 'Family and friends will be calling. I've arranged the funeral for Friday, here in the village. Just family will come back here for a little while. Perhaps you will discuss with Nel what arrangements are needed to be made. I thought that we might send Nanny on holiday for a few weeks…'

'You're not discharging her,' said Fran quickly. 'I'm so glad—she would break her heart.'

He said evenly, 'She's been with us since Lisa was a year old—she is part of the household.'

'And I'm not,' thought Fran miserably. As soon as he decently could he would arrange things so that she could go back to England.

She drank coffee and crumbled toast, mindful of his remark that they had nothing to say to each other.

Litrik's parents arrived during the morning, and then his sisters; they were warmly sympathetic and Mevrouw van Rijgen observed very positively that although Fran had been Lisa's stepmother for such a short time, she had brought the child a happiness she had hankered after. 'So you mustn't grieve too much, my dear,' she said kindly. 'It has been a sad blow to all of us, especially to Litrik, but happily you are here to comfort him.'

Fran was profoundly thankful that he wasn't there to hear his mother say that.

More people came, friends—old friends of Litrik's who, it seemed, had known him for years. Fran said all the right things, dispensed coffee and tea and longed for the day to be over. The visitors went at last and they dined together, carrying on a polite conversation, not a word of which did she remember later. She went to bed directly afterwards, pleading a headache, thankful that Litrik was going to the hospital in the morning and would be out all day.

She breakfasted alone and since he had already left the house she told Tuggs that she was going for a drive and presently got into the Mini and took the well-remembered road to the fairytale pond.

It was a sad autumn day, not raining but damp and grey, and the old woman wasn't in her garden. Fran got out of the car and knocked on the door and, bidden to enter, gave her sad news in her slowly improving Dutch.

The old woman nodded and smiled and patted her shoulder to show that she understood. She pushed a chair forward and urged Fran to sit down. *'Koffie,'* she said and trotted off to her tiny kitchen and came back presently with two cups and saucers on a tray, looking kindly into Fran's tired unhappy face. Presently she said, 'You can come here whenever you want to, Mevrouw.' And somehow that made Fran feel better; she didn't suppose that she would be in Holland much longer, but this funny little cottage was somewhere to come. She thanked the old woman and asked if she might walk to the pond.

There were damp leaves strewn all over the path now and the trees were looking woebegone, but the pond was still lovely even on such a sombre day. Fran sat down on the tree stump once more and looked at the still, grey water. She had never felt so lonely or so unhappy. She grieved for Lisa and she was saddened, too, because Litrik didn't want her or her sympathy. It was as though at the child's death, he had discarded her; she had fulfilled her part of their agreement and now he had no further interest in her... She sat up straight at her sudden astounding thought: he might not want any more to do with her, but the idea of never seeing him again struck her with sickening force. Without him life would never be the same any more. She was quite bewildered, for he behaved towards her at best as a casual friend and at worst as though he couldn't bear the sight of her. So how could she possibly love him? She reminded herself of his coldness, the faint mockery with which he looked at her, his total lack of interest in her as a person. That he had always behaved in exactly the right manner towards her when Lisa had been with them meant nothing; the happy picnics, the games of Ludo and Snakes and Ladders, the laughter and early morning teas, all of them had been to give Lisa happiness.

She watched the water coot weave in and out of the reeds and then disappear. In all fairness, she thought, when Litrik had made his astonishing proposal, he hadn't offered her friendship or even liking, only his promise that, when she returned to England, he would see that she would get a job again.

She shifted a bit more on the tree stump, feeling the chill creeping up her legs. But to be honest, she hadn't expected anything else from him, had she? And it had all seemed so simple and straightforward, hadn't it? But it wasn't any more. She had grown to love Lisa even in the short time that she had known her and as well as that she had grown to love Litrik's home; now there was nothing more she could ask of life than to stay there with him for the rest of her life and his. Only he didn't want her.

She got up and walked slowly back to where she had parked the car, waved goodbye to the old woman and drove back to the house. It was late afternoon by then; Tuggs brought her tea in the little sitting room and she sat with the dogs, thinking about Lisa and thinking of the future. She would have to stay for a little while after the funeral but there was nothing to stop her planning what she would do when she went back to England. Not to the aunts, of course; they would never understand in the first place. Sooner or later they would have to be told but not just yet. And she would try for a job in London and make a new life for herself.

Litrik came back for dinner. He asked her kindly enough if she had found the day trying, expressed relief that she had taken the car for a run and went on to talk about his work at the hospital. He didn't mention Lisa once, merely remarking as they crossed the hall to the drawing room for their coffee that he hoped that she and Nel had arranged things for Friday.

'Yes,' said Fran, 'everything is seen to.' And before she could add to that he went on, 'I've spoken to Nanny. She will take a few weeks' holiday starting on Saturday. Her home is in Friesland; Tuggs will drive her there.'

He was sitting in his chair by the fire and she thought with compassion that he looked every day of his age, his grief hidden under that bland mask of a face. She opened her mouth ready to pour out the sympathy she felt and then closed it again; they had nothing to say to each other—he had said that and she mustn't forget it. She had no idea that loving someone who wasn't even interested in you could hurt so much. They drank their coffee, not talking much, and presently he went away to his study.

It was raining when she got up in the morning and when she got downstairs Tuggs met her with the news that Litrik had gone in to the hospital at Zeist and she wasn't to expect him until the evening. 'A mercy that he is kept so busy, Mevrouw, if you'll pardon the liberty.' He gave her a worried look. 'Not a nice day for you to go out, Mevrouw.'

'No, I'll take the dogs for a walk and then I'll go over to Bloemendaal and see my cousin—I'll stay for lunch, Tuggs, but I'll be back round about tea time in case Nel wants any help. Everything is all right for tomorrow, isn't it?'

It was mid-morning by the time she got back with the dogs and had dried them and settled down in the small sitting room. Clare was in when she phoned and eager to see her; she got into her new Burberry and the smart little hat that went with it, put on some elegant shoes and drove off.

She hadn't told Clare about Lisa; that was something she would have to do during her visit with as little emotion as possible. Clare's baby was due in two months or so and she was living in a happy world of her own which it would be cruel to disturb.

She hadn't seen her cousin since the wedding although they had talked on the phone; Clare and Karel had been away staying with his parents and they wouldn't have heard of Lisa's death.

She parked the car and rang the bell and ran up the stairs to the flat, stifling a strong urge to pour out the whole unhappy business to Clare—she realised she couldn't do that; Dominee Meertens had said that only the three of them knew the true facts of the marriage… It wasn't her secret.

Clare was waiting at the open door and they hugged each other delightedly. 'Gosh, you look marvellous!' declared Fran. 'It's not too long now, is it?'

She cast off her raincoat and hat and her cousin eyed the suede outfit with envy. 'Well, look at you,' she declared, 'and those shoes—Fran, I hardly recognise you.' She gave Fran another look. 'Come in and have coffee—it's all ready, and you can tell me why you've lost weight and look as though you haven't slept for nights on end.'

Which made it easy for Fran to tell her about Lisa. 'It has upset us all,' she finished, 'and Litrik is broken-hearted—he adored her.' She paused. 'So did I.'

'What a mercy he married you,' observed Clare. 'You've got each other and that's all that matters, isn't it?' She gave Fran a long thoughtful look. 'So that's why you look so unhappy—you had me worried…'

Fran passed her cup for more coffee. She didn't want it, but it was something to do. 'And I want to know all about you and the baby—when is he due? Not long, surely?'

Clare was only too ready to talk about it and presently Fran was shown the baby's outfits and the dear little room Karel had decorated and fitted out.

'And once he is here, we shall come over and see you,' declared Clare happily. 'Will you be here for Christmas or will Litrik take you over to England? Not that it would be much fun to be with the aunts.'

'Well,' said Fran calmly, 'he's not said anything but then I hadn't expected him to; and he is very busy at the hospital—there have been several cases of legionnaire's disease and he specialises in tropical diseases and fevers, you know.'

She steered the talk back to the baby and Clare chatted happily until Fran said reluctantly that she would have to go.

'Oh, of course, Litrik gets back about tea time, I suppose, and you like to be there. Come and see me again, Fran.' Clare kissed her warmly. 'And next time you'll be your old self.'

Fran managed a laugh. 'Oh, dear, have I been such a wet blanket?'

'No, love—just unhappy and hiding it very well.'

It was a nasty afternoon turning rapidly into evening, with a cold rain falling steadily and a lot of traffic on the roads, even the country roads she took. It suited her mood; depression sat heavily upon her; the sight of Clare so happy, bubbling over with excitement about the baby, had filled her with an envy she didn't realise she possessed. It was impossible not to dream a little—to be happily married to Litrik who loved her and to have his babies. Fran, lost in her dream world, put out her right-hand indicator and turned left and was subjected to an indignant fanfare of horns.

She was surprised to find Litrik at home when she got in. She said awkwardly as he came into the hall, 'I spent the day with Clare. I didn't know you would be back before dinner.'

He took her raincoat and threw it over a chair. 'She is well, I hope?' he enquired politely, and stood aside for her to go into the drawing room. He spoke pleasantly and she did her best to follow his lead. 'Oh, fine—the baby's due in about eight weeks.' She sat down near the fire. 'What a wretched afternoon. I came home through the side roads and everything was very gloomy.'

He had come to sit opposite to her. 'I'll explain tomorrow's arrangements, shall I? Very simple, but it helps to know something about them beforehand.'

And during the next day, which was sad and difficult, she had been grateful for the things he had told her. They had helped her to play her part without faltering, act hostess to his family and friends and hide her own grief under a calm exterior. Only when everyone had gone and they were standing in the hall as Tuggs closed the doors on the last of the family, did she say suddenly and incoherently, 'You don't mind—I'd like to go—a headache…'

He had been so kind and thoughtful, perhaps only because there were other people there, but she didn't think so—it was as though he had understood at last that she was grieving for Lisa, too. But now she couldn't bear another minute of it. She had to get away and pull herself together. She loved him so much that she was terrified of showing it in some way and her longing to comfort him was almost unbearable. He had gone through the day with a calm face, courteous to everyone who had come, but now she wondered what he would do.

He answered her incoherent excuses with impersonal kindness. 'Of course you must be tired. I'll get Nel to send up something on a tray for you later on.'

She said quickly, 'I'll come down for dinner— you'll be alone…'

'I've a good deal to do—letters to write; I'll be too busy to miss you.' He smiled as he spoke, dismissing her, and she went to her room. Even if he weren't busy he wouldn't miss her, she thought drearily.

She didn't expect to sleep but she did and in the morning she felt better. Moping and moaning weren't going to help; she would have to pick up the threads of life again and wait patiently until Litrik considered it the right moment to get the annulment. It was no use trying to alter things; she had known exactly what he had planned from the very beginning and she had agreed with him. She hadn't been in love with him then, of course, which complicated things, but that was something she must learn to get over as soon as possible.

She dressed and went down to breakfast, outwardly serene. He would be away all day, he told her in the pleasant impersonal manner which chilled her so, and he would be flying to Brussels on the following day— a deliberate arrangement to get him away from home, she felt sure. Having to keep up the pretence of their marriage now that Lisa wasn't with them any more must be irksome to him. After all, her reason for being there in the first place had gone; she had no place with him any more. She replied suitably to his news, expressed the wish that his visit would be successful and asked in her matter-of-fact way if there was anything she could do for him while he was away.

There wasn't and there wasn't any way of being sure when he would be back. An answer she had expected anyway.

They were alone in the room and he bade her goodbye in a manner which put her very much in mind of his leave taking on her wards, pausing just long enough to tell her that if necessary he could be reached at the phone number he had left on his desk in the study.

She sat at the table, listening to him talking to Tuggs in the hall and then to the sound of the receding car. Tuggs came in then to see if there was anything she wanted and she told him briskly that she would take the dogs for a walk and then drive into Zeist to buy some embroidery wools.

'And I'll stay out for lunch, Tuggs. Shall I come and see Nel now?'

She went to the kitchen for her daily talk with that lady. Until now it had been brief, for Lisa demanded all her attention, but now there was time to learn a few useful words and pick up a few hints about the housekeeping, a waste of time really since she wouldn't be there for long enough to need them, but it kept her occupied.

She walked the dogs for an hour and then drove to Zeist, to potter round the shops there, drink coffee and then fill in another hour choosing knitting patterns until she could go to the Hermitage Hotel and have lunch.

She didn't drive straight back but meandered around the country roads, losing her way several times so that the afternoon was fading when she got home. The drawing room looked inviting and the dogs were glad to see her; Tuggs brought tea and she sat down by the fire, just for the moment enjoying an illusion of content, broken by Tuggs with the afternoon post. There was a letter from her aunts—she wrote to them weekly but they wrote seldom and when they did their letters unsettled her. They had a companion housekeeper now who apparently did nothing right and expected free evenings and a week-end off once a month, during which time, if Aunt

Kate was to be believed, the aunts starved, froze to death and suffered all the privations of being neglected. Fran sat with the letter on her lap when she had read it and wondered if she should go back and live there with them when she went back to England. Perhaps it was her duty; on the other hand, when she had lived with them they had found fault with her continuously and matters would not improve. Far better to go right away and start again. She began to think what she might do, resolutely refusing to dwell on a future without Litrik; her heart might be breaking but she must ignore that and no one need ever know. She was debating the advantages of a post in London in a teaching hospital against a job in Canada or New Zealand when Litrik walked in. She hadn't expected him to come home before dinner and she jerked up in her chair as the dogs went to meet him.

'I startled you. I'm sorry, Francesca.' His glance fell on the open letter in her lap. 'Letters from home?'

He had sat down on the other side of the fireplace with Muff draped over his feet and Thor sitting beside him. 'You've had a pleasant day?' he wanted to know.

'Yes, thank you. Would you like tea?'

He shook his head. 'I had a cup at the hospital.' He glanced at his watch. 'I must go again in an hour—a private patient at my rooms. Don't wait dinner for me. Perhaps you would ask Nel to leave something for me—sandwiches will do.'

She asked, 'Are you going to the hospital before you leave tomorrow? Will you want an early lunch?'

'I must leave here soon after six o'clock—I've a lecture to give in the morning. I'm catching an early plane from Schiphol.'

She said quietly, 'I see,' and then, because it was something to say, 'do you know Brussels well?'

'I have been there on various occasions.' He got up and fetched the small pile of letters on one of the tables and then sat down again. 'You don't mind if I read my post?'

'No,' said Fran and wished that she had her knitting with her. They were like two strangers who, having met for the first time, didn't like each other but felt impelled to make polite conversation. A waste of time, she thought, suddenly pettish, when we could be talking about Lisa and helping each other through this ghastly time. I could even have gone to Brussels with him…

She sat composedly, the picture of serenity, and the doctor, glancing at her over his letters, looked a second time before going back to his reading and then almost reluctantly looked at her again. He asked abruptly, 'You'll be all right while I'm away?'

That surprised her. 'Oh, yes, there are the dogs and so much to do…'

He looked a little taken aback. 'Much to do? What?'

'Well, as I said—the dogs. They like a good long walk, don't they? And then I talk to Nel about the meals and so on, and there are always letters to write and knitting to do and I can take the car to Zeist or Utrecht.'

'Do you miss your work at the hospital?' he asked abruptly.

'I didn't; perhaps I do now. You see, I've always...that is, a nurse's life is busy.'

'You don't dislike the idea of going back to it?'

'Not in the least.' Her voice was quite steady. Perhaps he was going to tell her that he'd see about the annulment. She shrank from hearing about it but at least he was talking to her.

She was to be disappointed; he put his letters aside and got up to go. 'Well, I must be off—I'll phone from Brussels before I leave there. Good night, Francesca.'

She wished him good night in a bright voice and only when she heard the car start did she get up and go upstairs to her room. She could howl her eyes out there in peace.

She felt much better after that; indeed a small well of indignation spread quite rapidly from somewhere deep inside her. She had done her best to keep her side of the bargain and he could have shown some gratitude, at least. Lisa's death had hit him hard, but it had made her very unhappy, too, and he hadn't seen that—but then he hardly ever looked at her...

She walked down to the village the next morning, put fresh roses from the garden on Lisa's grave and then had coffee with Dominee Meertens and his wife.

The house was quieter now for the children were in school and they sat comfortably in the rather untidy sitting room, talking in a pleasant desultory fashion until Mevrouw Meertens asked, 'Did you not want to go with Litrik? He would have been glad of your company.'

Before Fran could answer the *dominee* said, 'Well, he would have very full days. I imagine it would hardly be worth your going, Francesca?'

She agreed and threw him a grateful glance. Perhaps she could have a real talk with him sometime and find out what Litrik proposed to do and when.

She spent the afternoon at the piano and after her solitary dinner went to bed early.

Litrik didn't telephone for three days; he would be back for dinner that evening, he told her over the phone and, after a polite enquiry as to her well being, rang off. It was unfortunate that his mother had been driven over for a brief afternoon visit and was sitting near enough for her to hear Fran's side of the conversation, businesslike yeses and noes and no endearments of any sort. When Fran had sat down again Mevrouw van Rijgen passed her cup for more tea and remarked, 'Is Litrik a difficult husband, my dear? Not that you are likely to tell me. His first marriage was so unhappy you know; he became so—so remote, and now losing Lisa has upset him badly. We had hoped that when he married you it would help him to accept the fact that she was dying and to regain his happiness.' She hesitated. 'A happy home life and children... He is very fond of children.'

Fran poured herself more tea. She said in a calm voice, 'I think it's early days for Litrik to feel better about Lisa—he loved her very much and even though he had known for months that there was no hope for her, it was still a dreadful shock. We all miss her, you know. I wish I had known her for longer.'

'Yes, well, my dear...I dare say a few weeks spent quietly here with you will help him. It has been hard to talk to him since his first marriage broke up; you are a sweet girl and gentle and I think you will succeed where the rest of us have failed.' She added abruptly, 'He can be unkind but I believe that he doesn't mean it.'

She put down her cup and got up. 'I must go home. I've enjoyed our little chat, Francesca. Give my love to Litrik when he gets back, and tell him we hope to see you both soon.'

She kissed Fran with warmth and went out to the waiting car, leaving her to ponder over their talk. Did Litrik's mother suspect that things weren't quite as they should be with a newly married couple? Not that it mattered now, very soon they would part and once she was back in England she would be forgotten in a few months' time. They would be very kind about it; an unfortunate mistake made by both of them and luckily dealt with in time before there were any children. Finally she fell to daydreaming over little Litriks and their sisters running round the house, rushing to meet a devoted Papa each evening while she stood, presently to be held close and kissed.

She dressed carefully for Litrik's return and went to sit in the drawing room with the tapestry work she had started. He came in quietly and she paused with her needle poised to say serenely, 'Hallo, Litrik. I hope you had a successful time in Brussels and a good journey back.'

It sounded very stilted in her eyes, but it was either that or jumping up and flinging herself into his arms and that wouldn't do at all.

He went to pour a drink and offered her sherry before he sat down opposite her. 'Have you been lonely?' he asked abruptly.

She answered him evasively. 'I've had a visit from your mother—she came to tea. And I went to Dominee Meertens and had coffee. The weather's been quite nice; that meant the dogs and I have been able to walk miles.'

'You haven't answered my questions.'

She took a couple of stitches very precisely. 'One doesn't have to be alone to be lonely,' she told him coolly.

'While I was away I had time to think. I've treated you badly, Francesca, and I'm sorry. You were sad and I did nothing to help you. It's been a difficult time and I made it worse for you. I'm grateful for what you have done and you did it splendidly.'

She glanced at him. 'I loved Lisa,' she said baldly.

'Yes, I know.' He bent to stroke Muff's ears and

then throw an arm round Thor. 'Francesca, there is
something you are entitled to know. I have told no
one else and don't intend to. Lisa wasn't my daughter.' And, at Fran's sudden surprised gasp, 'No, don't
say anything yet. My first wife had an affair before
we married unknown to me. She was pregnant then.
It wasn't until some weeks later that I found out quite
by chance that she had done her best to get rid of the
child without my knowledge. She failed but Lisa was
born handicapped. Her mother would have nothing to
do with her—rejected her completely and left us both.
I swore then that Lisa would have every possible
chance to live and be happy. She has been my first
concern since then.'

'Why did she marry you?' whispered Fran.
'Couldn't she have married the father?'

'He had no money. I happen to be wealthy, I was
also infatuated.'

'And her mother?' Fran's voice was still a shocked
whisper.

'Has been dead for five years.'

'And you still love her?'

He looked at her with hard eyes. 'I never loved
her—love and infatuation are two quite different
things. Love to my mind, is something one reads
about—a myth…'

'That's rubbish!' said Fran sharply. 'What about
your parents and your sisters and Dominee Meertens
and his wife and Clare and Karel? Of course it's not

a myth and if you loved someone you wouldn't talk such nonsense.'

He smiled at her mockingly. 'Why, Francesca, one might almost think that you were speaking from experience.'

She saw that he considered it so ridiculous that there was no need to be serious about it. She said merely, 'I use my eyes,' and changed the subject abruptly. 'Your mother hopes to see you soon.'

'We'll go over this weekend. Was my father with her?'

Fran shook her head. 'No, he had to attend some meeting or other.'

'They like you...'

'I'm glad of that.' She chose some wool with care and threaded her needle. He went on deliberately, 'And I find that I like you, too, Francesca, though unwillingly.'

Her heart rocked against her ribs. 'Then when we part we shall be able to do so in a friendly fashion.' She gave him a considered look. 'When is that to be, Litrik?'

'I have thought about that, too—I think we must wait a little while longer.' He was staring at her so hard that she felt the colour creeping into her cheeks. She didn't look away. 'I'm quite ready to go when you want me to.' She folded her work and laid it on the table by her chair.

'There's the gong—I expect you are hungry?'

Dinner passed off well enough; Litrik when he

chose could be an amusing companion. They went back to the drawing room for their coffee and Fran, not wishing to push her luck, went to bed shortly afterwards. Litrik had seemed to enjoy her company; he had confided in her, admitted that he liked her; it wasn't much, but it was better than the cold silences she had had to put up with. She would have to leave, of course, but at least not just yet. For that she was thankful. Every single minute of his company was something to treasure for the future.

CHAPTER EIGHT

A WEEK went by, during which Litrik came home for lunch each day and returned in the early evening and even, on two occasions, for tea. They had gone to lunch with his parents, sustained an unexpected afternoon visit from Tante Olda and Tante Nynke, on their stately way to visit friends in Valkenburg, and had Professor van Tromp, a large quiet man who said little, to dinner. He and Litrik wandered off after dinner to the latter's study. They returned full of apologies; they had had a most interesting discussion, he explained to her, and begged her forgiveness. 'But of course, being a doctor's wife you will understand,' he ended kindly and drank the coffee she had ready for them and took his leave, inviting her at the same time to visit the hospital if she should care to do so. 'Although I dare say Litrik has been badgering you to do so already.'

As they went back into the drawing room Fran asked thoughtfully, 'Why don't you? Invite me to see round your hospitals—and your consulting rooms? Wives are supposed to take an interest in their husband's work, aren't they?' And, when he didn't answer, 'I am a little tired of this pretence and surely you must be, too. When Lisa was alive there was a reason for it.'

She was standing in the centre of the room, looking at him. 'How long does it take—an annulment, I mean?'

His voice was very even. 'A little while—we must talk about it.'

She had been feeling off colour all the evening, now her head began to ache most vilely. Perhaps because of that she snapped, 'No, we mustn't. You said that we had nothing to say to each other.' She walked to the door murmuring a good night, longing for her bed. For some reason the staircase was unending; by the time she reached the gallery above she was worn out and icy cold. She undressed quickly, her head hammering so hard now that all she could think of was getting into bed. She was sliding into its comfort when she got out again, put on her dressing-gown and went back into the gallery, making for the stairs. She felt ill, but at the same time there was something that she simply had to say to Litrik. She reached the staircase and started down it. Her head was a ball of fire, some demon was pouring ice water down her spine, her legs had no bones. Halfway down she paused; the stairs spread away from her, curiously flattened so that she wasn't certain where the next tread was. She put out a cautious foot, missed a step and tumbled headlong.

Litrik, in his study, with a pile of notes before him, ignored them, seeing instead a pair of lovely eyes in a tired face, and listening to a regrettably snappy voice telling him strongly that they had nothing to say to each other. He frowned as his thoughts were interrupted by a series of soft gentle bumps and the slithering of Fran's small person. He got up and went into the hall; it was past midnight and the house had been silent for some time.

Fran lay in an untidy heap, almost at the bottom of the staircase. She had knocked herself out, which was a pity, otherwise she would have heard—even if she hadn't believed—Litrik's, 'Fran—my dear little Fran,' uttered in a voice quite unlike his usual cool tones.

There was a reddened bump already visible on her forehead which told its own tale. He lifted her eyelids and looked into her eyes, took her pulse, made sure that there were no broken bones, then scooped her up and carried her upstairs to her room, where he put her on the bed, took off her dressing-gown and tucked her up. Only then did he go to the bell-pull by the fireplace and give it a sharp tug. There wouldn't be anyone in the kitchen at that time of night, but the Tuggs had their sitting room only a short distance from it and the bell was loud. While he waited he went back to the bed and took another look at Fran. Her face was pale and the bump was getting bigger but that wouldn't account for her obvious high fever.

He began to examine her carefully and when Tuggs, cosily dressing-gowned, came into the room he said, 'Get my bag from the study will you, Tuggs, and then go to the kitchen and get some ice and some cloths to put in it. My wife has knocked herself out falling down the stairs, but I believe she has some kind of infection.'

Tuggs, beyond a worried 'Tut tut', wasted no time on words. He was back in no time at all with the bag and went away again without a word.

Fran's temperature was high enough to make Litrik raise his eyebrows. He studied her face carefully in an impersonal and professional manner, sure that the concussion was secondary to the sudden high fever. He got up and shaded the bedside light carefully, pulled a chair close to the bed and, when Tuggs came back, wrapped ice in the linen hand towels he had brought, and held it over her forehead. He didn't look up as Nel came quietly in to stand beside him. She spoke in a whisper and he listened patiently and shook his head, answering her softly, and presently, after an anxious peer at Fran, she went away to get the coffee he had asked for.

'And Tuggs, will you go to my study and bring up the papers on my desk—the pile in the centre in a folder.'

'You'll stay here, sir?' Tuggs hesitated. 'Me and Nel will gladly sit with Mevrouw.'

'Thank you, Tuggs, I know you would, but I'll stay just to make sure she is all right when she comes round. She will probably be sick and feel peculiar; perhaps it'll make things easier if I'm here. You both go back to bed—I'll get you on the house phone if I need you'. He glanced at the faithful Tuggs. 'Don't worry—my wife's picked up a virus infection I believe—that's how she came to fall downstairs. A few days in bed will put her right again.'

It took more than a few days. Fran came round in the early hours of the morning to see Litrik sitting by her bed, writing busily. She still had a fearful headache; indeed, the whole of her ached but her head felt clearer. He had looked up and seen her eyes open and on him and got to his feet and come to take her pulse and feel her hot forehead. 'That's better,' he told her soothingly. 'I'm going to give you something for the headache I'm quite certain you've got, and you'll go to sleep again and feel better by morning.'

He had turned her pillow and it felt blessedly cool to her poor hot head and he asked her if she wanted a drink, and offered her something in a medicine glass, and then another drink, and she had slept again, to wake in the morning feeling almost sensible once more, but disinclined to so much as turn her head on the pillow. When she saw him still sitting in the chair she muttered, 'Have you been there all night? You must go to bed—I'm quite all right now, but if you don't mind I don't think I'll get up just yet.'

His low laugh made her frown. 'You won't get up until I tell you that you may, Francesca, and I warn you that if you do you will fall flat on your face. I shall go away presently and Nel or one of the maids will be here.'

He got up and went to the door. 'I shall be home

for lunch. Tuggs will take any calls. Nel will give you something to bring down the fever; drink as much as you can manage.'

He might just have finished a ward round, thought Fran drowsily.

Incredibly, it was more than a week before she crept from her bed, sat in an easy chair, and crept thankfully back again. The concussion hadn't been severe; the bump had subsided, leaving a yellow and purple bruise, but the virus had taken longer to go, and it had taken a good deal of the energy she possessed with it. But despite her small size she was strong and healthy and within a few days of getting up again she was downstairs, rather pale and a good deal thinner.

Litrik had visited her daily morning and evening, sitting down by her bed to tell her any small items of family news and read her the many letters written by his family, as well as long screeds from Clare and the brief stiff letters from the aunts, flavoured with the faint suggestion that if she chose to marry a foreigner and live on the continent, she must expect to fall a prey to unpleasant illnesses. She had chuckled weakly at this and Litrik laughed with her.

His father and mother came to visit her, as did Jebbeke and Wilma, and, since the weather was fine even if cold, she was wrapped up warmly by Nel and taken for short drives by Litrik. It was three weeks before she felt herself again, and once more went walking with the dogs and going down to the village to visit

Dominee Meertens and his wife. It was on one of these visits, while his wife was out of the room with the idea of fetching the coffee, that she asked diffidently if Litrik had said anything to him about the annulment.

'Yes, he has.' The *dominee*'s booming voice had sunk to a discreet level. 'And at a suitable moment I have no doubt he will speak to you, Francesca.'

She had to be content with that; she had the sense to know that Litrik wouldn't have said anything while she was ill and she had been thankful for that, shutting her mind to her inevitable departure.

But Litrik said nothing. They began to go out and about again to friends for dinner, to the theatre and even, to her surprise, to the hospital in Utrecht, where she had a guided tour of the hospital while Litrik delivered a lecture to a hall full of students, coming to collect her in Theatre Sister's office, where he sat drinking coffee and behaving in a manner which she imagined an attentive husband might. She had been bewildered for there was really no need for him to go to such lengths.

The next afternoon she drove the Mini to see the old woman. It was a blustery day with grey clouds scudding across a cold blue sky, but the old woman, muffled in an old coat, was working in her garden. She stuck her fork in the ground when she saw Fran getting out of the car and came down the path to meet her. It took Fran a moment or two to unravel the old woman's Dutch. Her knowledge of that language was getting better by the day and she could at least make herself understood. Her companion nodded sympathetically as Fran explained her long absence, invited her to drink a cup of coffee and suggested that while it was being prepared perhaps she would like to walk to the pond. Even on such a dreary day as this, said the old woman, it was beautiful. She spoke proudly as though she owned the pond, which, reflected Fran, perhaps she did. She nodded her acceptance of the coffee and went out of the garden and along the path between the bushes and trees, mostly bare now, until she came to the pond. The old woman was right, it was beautiful, its water reflecting the stormy sky, its banks littered with fallen leaves. And the tree stump was still there; Fran sat down on it. Perhaps Lisa's happy little ghost was beside her; certainly her memory was vivid. She sat for a few minutes, grateful for the peaceful quiet all around her and presently went back to the cottage where she drank her coffee and carried on a muddled but animated conversation with her hostess.

She couldn't stay long, Litrik would be back before six o'clock and she had made a point of being home when he got in. When Lisa had been alive he had come home in time for tea if he possibly could, but now he had taken to staying at his consulting rooms each afternoon. There was, after all, no need for him to hurry home any more.

She saw very little of him; breakfast was never a protracted meal and if he was in for lunch that, too, was by no means a leisurely meal. Only in the evenings would he sit with her before dinner, talking pleasantly about nothing that mattered, making small talk at the table and then, when they had had coffee, going to his study. She saw more of him if friends or family came to dinner or they went out, but although she longed to be with him, the effort of hiding her real feelings was getting a bit too much.

She bade the old woman goodbye, promised to return in two days' time and drove home.

It was the following week, her fourth visit since she had been ill, that she arrived at the cottage to find no sign of the old woman. Her two cats were sitting on the doorstep, looking anxious, and there was no smoke coming from the chimney. Fran walked up the little path, looking around her. The garden fork was stuck in the earth beside a row of carrots, half dug, and the cats, when she reached them, looked hungry. She knocked on the door and heard nothing in the silence all around her. She knocked again and this time she did hear something, a weary rending cough.

'Bronchitis,' said Fran to the cats, her nurse's instincts taking over, and she tried the door. It opened. The cats shot past her into the tiny lobby. The little sitting room was empty and cold; she went into the kitchen and at once saw the old woman huddled on a chair by the old-fashioned pot stove, now out. She looked ill and exhausted and when she tried to speak coughed instead so that Fran begged her to save her breath. It would take too long to ask her slowly thought out questions and then puzzle out the answers. She filled a kettle at the old-fashioned stone sink, lighted the Calor gas ring and found the coffee pot. She found milk, too, in an icy little pantry, put some on to heat, and then gave the cats each a saucerful.

Between bouts of coughing the old woman drank a cupful of coffee and Fran was relieved to see a little colour creeping back into her cheeks. She sought feverishly for the Dutch for blanket and dredged it up from the back of her head with great relief. The old woman pointed a feeble hand towards the ceiling and Fran climbed the ladderlike narrow stairs and found an attic above, one corner boarded off to make a bedroom of sorts. There were blankets here; she took two and made her precarious way back down the stairs and tucked them round her patient and then set about dealing with the stove. There was an empty bucket beside it. She picked it up and went outside and round the cottage to the back where there were some broken-down sheds. There was a small pile of egg coals there, some small logs and several broken wooden boxes. Firewood, said Fran happily, and found a lethal looking axe propped against the wall with which she attacked the boxes. She wasn't very expert but she was desperate to get the house warm. Armed with her bucket of coal and the wood she went back indoors, cleaned the stove as best she could and laid the fire, following her companion's muttered instructions very carefully. The stove obliged, roaring up the flue pipe in an alarming manner until, obedient to the old woman's urgent directions, she opened this and shut that and added more coal.

It was growing dark and she lit the oil lamp on the kitchen table, washed her grimy hands and found a basin. The old woman wasn't too keen on being washed, but she looked a little better by the time Fran had sponged her face and hands and presently dozed off, waking for coughing bouts and dropping off again. 'Food,' said Fran to the cats and remembered the hens the old woman kept—she and Lisa had seen them on one of their visits scratching contentedly in a wired-in enclosure behind the cottage. They would need to be fed and the eggs collected; she had no idea how long the old woman had been ill but she began to doubt if she had been able to cope with the hens. Fran went quietly out of the house again and explored the sheds. In one of them she found a sack of what she hoped was chicken feed. She filled a dipper and made her way to the hens, who rushed to the wire as soon as they saw her and fell to with a good deal of clucking. There was an egg box behind the chicken house; she opened it cautiously and found eggs. 'Egg and milk,' said Fran, and sped back to the cottage.

Her patient was still in uneasy sleep. She got the egg and milk ready, found some stale bread in an earthen crock, warmed more milk and gave it to the cats. The kitchen was warm now and, by the lamp's light, looked quite cosy. Dusk had slipped into darkness and she drew the curtains over the one window.

The old-fashioned wall clock struck seven as she did so and she was shocked at the chimes. There was no way of letting anyone know where she was; the old woman couldn't be left even for the short time it would take her to drive back to the village and try to find a phone. She would have to spend the night and hope that someone would go past the cottage in the early morning. The old lady woke and Fran coaxed some of the egg and milk down her reluctant throat, and, when she could take no more, gave the rest to the cats and went to fetch more of the egg coals. The stove smelled vilely but the warmth had revived the old woman; if she could keep her going until the morning... Fran sat down on one of the hard wooden chairs at the table, thankful that for the moment, at least, her patient was asleep.

Presently she told herself she would warm up the coffee, it would keep her awake. The cats had curled up on the blankets, cocooning their mistress, and for the moment there was nothing for her to do except think how angry Litrik would be.

In this she was mistaken. He had arrived home at his usual hour to find Tuggs looking anxious. 'It's Mevrouw, sir—always home by now and no sign of her...'

'Where did she go?' Litrik sounded calm.

'Well, that's the worry—I don't know. When Lisa was alive they used to go off together, ever so happy, some afternoons, and they always got back before five o'clock. And for the last week or so Mevrouw has driven off at just the same time and come back here soon after four o'clock.'

'And you've no idea where they—she goes?'

Tuggs shook his head.

Litrik was putting on his car coat again. 'I remember that it was mentioned one day—a secret they told me, but that was all. Do you suppose that anyone in the house has any idea?'

Tuggs slid away through the baize door into the kitchen regions and the doctor stood motionless, staring at the wall before him. Presently Tuggs came back with Bep, the elder of the two young maids who did the housework. She was a sensible girl. 'Yes,' she said, in answer to Litrik's questions, 'once, when they got back a bit later than usual and it had been raining, I helped them with their wet things and they were talking. A fairy pool they were talking of, and an old woman in a cottage.'

The doctor thanked her gravely, told Tuggs to get the car out again and went to his study, where he spread a map on his desk and studied it carefully. He found what he sought presently, picked up his bag and went out to the car where Tuggs was waiting.

'It's a long shot, Tuggs, but worth a try. Stay here, I'll phone you if I need you.' He paused. 'And if there are any messages make a careful note of them.'

Tuggs voiced the doctor's thought. 'If there's been an accident, sir, we'd have heard by now.'

Litrik nodded, got into the car and drove away. He knew the surrounding country well, he reached the crossroads and turned down the narrow lane and went slowly through the village. Half a mile further his headlights picked out the Mini parked untidily on the side of the lane.

He parked behind the Mini, leaving his lights on, took his bag from the car and went up the garden path.

There was a faint glimmer of light coming from somewhere inside and then the sound of someone coughing. He knocked on the door and when no one came, knocked again, this time loudly and at length. He was rewarded by the glimmer of light becoming stronger and then Fran's voice calling in her slow Dutch, 'Who's there?'

'Litrik—open up, Francesca.'

The door was flung open and Fran with the lamp in her hand stood gazing up at him. She said breathlessly, 'Thank God you've come! How did you know? She's ill, the old woman who lives here, and I don't know what to do...'

He crowded into the tiny lobby, kissed her fiercely, took the lamp from her and went into the kitchen, where he set the lamp on the table, took off his coat and went to look at the old woman, awake now and looking bewildered.

He treated her very gently, asked her quiet questions while he took her pulse and temperature and, without disturbing the cats, contrived to go over her chest with his stethoscope. Then he wrapped her up again, gave her a reassuring pat and turned to Fran.

'So, tell me all you know and what you've done.'

So she told him and when she had finished he nodded. 'You did well. It's bronchitis and she tells me she refuses to leave here. I'm going back to the village to find someone to come out here and look after her. I'll phone Tuggs at the same time. Everyone at the house is beside themselves about you.'

But not you, thought Fran silently, though all she said was, 'I'm sorry to have worried them. What do you want me to do?'

He smiled a little. 'What a practical girl you are. What is upstairs?'

'An attic and a bedroom boarded off. There is a second bed in the attic.'

'See if you can find any sheets and blankets and make up the beds. I'm going to give her an antibiotic now. Provided she will stay in bed for a few days I think she will recover. Is there any food in the house?'

'The eggs I fetched, some milk and stale bread. There's not much coal—it's that pressed coal dust. Oh, and nothing for the cats.'

'I'll tell Tuggs. Now come and hold this arm for me.'

The house was very quiet when he had gone. She sped up the stairs once more and poked her nose by the light of a candle into a cupboard in the attic and found sheets and blankets and an old eiderdown. She took them all downstairs again and spread them round the stove and went back to look for the old woman's night clothes—a voluminous nightie, spotlessly clean,

and a thick shawl. She found towels, too, and a jug
and basin and an old-fashioned stone hot water bottle.

It took a little time to take all the bedclothes upstairs again and boil the water for the bottle but that
done she set to to make up the beds, wrap the nightie
round the bottle and bury it into the bedclothes. She
went downstairs then and saw that Litrik had been
gone for almost an hour. The old woman was awake
again and coughing. Fran heated more milk and got
her to take it, and was thankful to hear the car stopping in the lane.

Litrik had someone with him, a middle-aged
woman with a long face and bright blue eyes, who
shook her hand as he said, 'This is Juffrouw de Wit;
she lives in the village on her own. I suppose one
would call her a girl Friday in England. She is sensible and willing to stay until Mevrouw Honig is better. Tuggs is coming over with food and so on. Have
you made up the beds?'

'Yes, but there is only one hot water bottle.'

'Tuggs is bringing one with him.' He went to bend
over his patient while Juffrouw smiled widely at Fran
and took off her coat and carefully removed a hard
felt hat from her head. Fran thought she would have
made an excellent nurse.

The two of them went upstairs then and Litrik followed with Mevrouw Honig in his arms, and left them
to get their patient undressed and into her warm
nightie and shawl and sitting comfortably against the
pillows Fran had found. It wasn't so cold in the attic

now; the chimney breast took up a good deal of the attic wall and was beginning to warm it. Mevrouw Honig coughed and sighed and dozed off, leaving Fran and Juffrouw de Wit to tidy up and go back to the kitchen. Litrik had fetched more coal and stoked up the stove. He was in his waistcoat and shirt sleeves, washing his hands at the sink, when there was a knock at the door. 'Tuggs,' he said over his shoulder. 'Let him in, please, Francesca.'

Tuggs beamed at her as he edged past, carrying a big box. 'We've all been in such a state, Mevrouw—what a relief to know you are safe and sound. Is this the kitchen?'

He put the box on the table and Fran and Juffrouw de Wit unpacked it. The contents were all that was most needed: milk and fresh bread, a simple dish of sliced meat, neatly covered, for Juffrouw de Wit, an egg custard, tea and coffee, sugar, tins of soup and a packet of scraps of things suitable for the cats. There were candles, too, and soap and a bottle of Dettol. Juffrouw looked her satisfaction and began to tidy everything away into the pantry, and Litrik put on his jacket and shrugged on his coat. He went upstairs then to take another look at his patient and when he came down gave Juffrouw de Wit the antibiotic pills which would have to be taken and his instructions as to the care of Mevrouw Honig. Fran, listening, made out that he would pay a visit on the next day.

They drove back then, Tuggs leading with Fran just

behind him and Litrik last of all. They caused quite a stir going through the village.

It was nice to be fussed over as she went into the house. Nel with Bep and Corrie, the younger maid, had formed a kind of welcoming committee to take her outdoor things and exclaim over her, even though she didn't understand all they said. She went up to her room and took a look at herself in the looking-glass. Then she saw that she looked frightful; her face was grimy and her hair hung in wisps and her dress was smeared in coal dust. She washed and did her hair, changed her dress and went downstairs and found Litrik waiting for her. He handed her a glass of sherry, remarking that she looked as though she needed it, which remark, considering that she had just spent ten minutes improving her appearance, was unfortunate. She drank the sherry rather fast and it went straight to her head. She had had no tea and it was now late evening and she was famished. She blinked away a sudden vagueness in her surroundings and Litrik, watching her, observed blandly, 'I dare say you're hungry, but would you like another sherry first?'

The look she gave him was so unhappy that he put his glass down and took her hands in his.

'Francesca—what is it? Do you not feel well? What's wrong?'

Everything was wrong; she was tired, she was hungry and she was hopelessly in love with a man who didn't care a row of pins about her. But, of course, she couldn't tell him that. 'How did you know where I was?' she asked.

He didn't appear to have noticed that she hadn't answered his questions.

'Bep remembered hearing Lisa talking to you about a cottage and a fairy pond; I know the country round here and I had a map—it wasn't difficult.'

He didn't tell her that he had sweated with fear, imagining her overcome by disaster and him unable to find her. He had been beside himself under his calm.

He let her hands go. 'There's the gong. You must be as famished as I am.'

It was long past their normal dinner hour but Nel had succeeded in offering a delicious meal. Fran listened to Litrik's easy talk about nothing much and answered when she should. It wasn't until he told her that Nanny, who hadn't come back from her holiday because of her mother's illness, was coming back on the following day that she smiled.

'Oh, I'm glad and I'm sure that Nel and the girls must have missed her. What will she do now that...?' She stopped.

'Lisa isn't here,' finished Litrik. 'Nel has plenty for her to do, so Tuggs tells me. Nel wants to see you about it—pickling and jam making and so on.'

Fran said slowly, 'There's no need to see me. I mean, Nel has been housekeeper here for years, hasn't she? And since I'll be gone...'

'Ah yes, but perhaps you would like to stay until the New Year? Have you anything in mind?'

'Well, no.' She added a little desperately, 'But I'd like to go as soon as you can arrange everything.'

He made no attempt to persuade her to say that she would stay. They went back to the drawing room and he told her, rather unnecessarily she thought, about the splendid Christmas and New Year celebrations. 'Everyone comes here,' he told her smoothly, 'we have a great tree in this room and the whole house is decorated and Nel turns out the most delicious food. Friends call and we give a party at New Year, and if it's cold enough we skate. A pity you won't be here to enjoy it all.'

She couldn't bear any more of that; she went to bed but before she went she asked, 'Do you want me to go and see Mevrouw Honig tomorrow?'

'I'll be home to lunch and I've no appointments until after four o'clock. We'll both go.'

He opened the door for her and as she went through she paused, her tongue uttering the words she had no intention of saying. 'Why did you kiss me like that?'

He didn't smile. 'An unavoidable reaction,' he observed. 'Good night, Francesca.'

In bed, curled up between fine linen sheets, she thought of Mevrouw Honig and Juffrouw de Wit and wondered what would have happened if she hadn't gone to the cottage that afternoon. It would have been nice if Litrik had said something kind about her hard work there, for it had been hard work. If she had been a dainty blond with big blue eyes and a helpless manner he would have praised her to the skies; as it was he took her for granted. She went to sleep on a wave of self-pity.

The morning was taken up with settling Nanny in again and hearing her news and then going to the kitchen to agree to Nel's suggestions about pickles and jams, and after lunch she got into the Daimler beside Litrik and was driven to the cottage.

It was one of those days when approaching winter allowed a forgotten autumn day to take over. The sun shone and although it was chilly there was little wind. They went up the path together and Juffrouw de Wit opened the door, her long face wreathed in smiles.

They were ushered into the small front room, very clean and neat but cold since there was no fire in the stove. But fortunately Litrik said that he would see his patient at once and at the same time swept Fran into the kitchen where Juffrouw de Wit had hurried to make coffee. It was warm there and Fran sat down at the table and listened to her companion's account of the night. All was well, she was told, Mevrouw Honig had slept fairly well and the cough seemed less severe. The doctor would be pleased…

He came down the precipitous stairs presently, ducking his head to avoid knocking himself out in the doorway, and accepted coffee while he listened to Juffrouw de Wit repeating everything she had said to Fran.

He allowed himself to be cautiously optimistic, he

told Fran; the old woman was better but would need several days in bed still. Then he turned his attention to Juffrouw de Wit once more, listening patiently to what she had to say, and then writing down fresh instructions.

'Is she all right for food?' asked Fran.

It seemed that someone had walked from the village that morning and brought milk and groceries with them. There was enough and to spare, declared Juffrouw de Wit.

They sat for a little while before Fran went up to see Mevrouw Honig. The antibiotic was already doing good work, the old woman was a better colour and she smiled at Fran and muttered something and Fran mustered her Dutch and wished the old woman a speedy recovery.

She and Litrik went down the garden under Juffrouw de Wit's approving eyes and as she went through the gate Fran asked, 'Would you like to see the fairy pool? I think Lisa would like that.'

He cast her a quick tender look, which she didn't see. 'I should like that.'

She led the way along the path and when the pond came into view she stopped for him to catch up with her. It was very quiet and the only movement was from the water coots on the far side of the pond.

'We always sat on that tree stump,' said Fran and two tears ran down her cheeks. She put up a gloved hand and wiped them away and blinked hard to hold back the rest of them, sniffing like a child. Litrik took a snowy handkerchief from a pocket and turned her round and mopped her face and she took it from him and blew her nose in a resolute fashion and said steadily, 'I am sorry, I didn't mean to cry. We were always happy here.' She looked up at him. 'You're not angry because we didn't share it with you?'

He stared down at her for a long moment and then shook his head. 'When I asked you to marry me it was because I wanted Lisa to have all the happiness she could before she died. You gave her that happiness; how could I possibly be angry?'

She watched a coot slide into the reeds just below them, and said sadly, 'I was happy, too...'

He asked abruptly, 'But not any more. I had wondered?'

'Well, everything is a bit uncertain, isn't it? I feel a fraud now, that is why I'd like to go.' She added politely, 'When it's convenient.' She looked around her and then back at his quiet face. 'It's been like a dream, hasn't it? But dreams end and we have to go our separate ways again.'

'You want that Francesca?'

'Yes, oh yes, I do... You must see...'

He said very quietly, 'You want to go back to nursing—to your old life in England? If that is your wish, then I will do all I can to help you.' He turned to leave the pool. 'Dreams don't have to end,' he said.

She wasn't really listening, which was a pity; her mind was already busy with the ways and means of getting a job. Not London—something remote, pref-

erably in the country where she could find her way
back to her old life once more. When that was done
she could go to London and get a good post and make
nursing her career. She sighed at the very idea and
Litrik turned to look at her.

'Don't worry, Francesca, you shall go just as soon
as I can arrange it. You may have to come back
briefly for the annulment but I'll do all I can to make
things easy for you.'

She turned to take a final look at the pool. She
could hardly see it through her tears.

CHAPTER NINE

LITRIK didn't come into the house with her, but drove off straight away to Utrecht, saying he would be home shortly before dinner, so she had a solitary tea by the fire and then went in search of Nanny who had elected to repair the tapestry on one of the massive armchairs in the drawing room. She was a clever needlewoman and, as she pointed out to Fran, only too glad to make herself useful. 'Until such time as I can be a nanny again,' she added and looked hopefully at Fran.

Fran bent over the chair, hiding her red face, murmuring vaguely. These were the awkward moments Litrik hadn't troubled to consider; they cropped up all the time and each time she felt like blurting out the truth. She began, a little feverishly, to talk to Nanny about Clare and the expected baby, a successful red herring which got her through the next five minutes and out of the room, with the excuse that she must walk the dogs.

She walked for miles, thinking about Litrik's promise that she could return to England as soon as he could arrange it. He hadn't sounded in the least put out about it; perhaps he was relieved that she had brought the subject up—it would have been an awkward subject for him to broach. All the same, he might have shown some regret. She turned for home, determined to start her packing as soon as possible so that she could go immediately he had arranged her journey.

To be thwarted within half an hour of his return home. Great Aunt Olda would be celebrating her eightieth birthday in four days time and the whole family would foregather to make it an occasion. Naturally, he pointed out, they would go. The great aunts lived to the north of Leeuwarden in the village of Rinsumaard, something over a hundred miles. He had arranged to be free on that day, they could drive up for lunch and return after dinner in the evening. And perhaps she would go into Utrecht with him and choose a suitable present.

She went with him the following morning since he wasn't due at the hospital until after lunch and spent an absorbing hour in a jeweller's shop choosing a diamond brooch for Tante Olda. Its price staggered Fran but, as Litrik pointed out, one wasn't eighty years old more than once and such an event called for something special. He took her to lunch after that, to Smits Hotel, and then drove her back home before returning to the hospital.

She suggested diffidently on their way back that she might get out the Mini and visit Mevrouw Honig and he agreed readily. 'I shall be going to see her tomorrow some time, but I'm sure she will be glad to see you. Could you find out if Juffrouw de Wit has all she wants? Anything she needs I can take with me tomorrow. And take a look at Mevrouw Honig, will you, and let me know how she is. Juffrouw de Wit is a worthy soul, but she isn't a trained nurse.'

So Fran got into the Mini and drove herself over to the cottage, to be met by Juffrouw de Wit with a most satisfactory report of her patient's progress. Certainly the old woman seemed better; beginning to eat again, said Juffrouw de Wit cheerfully, and taking her pills regularly. Fran checked her temperature and pulse and saw that her breathing was easier; the worst was over and she would be able to give Litrik a good report when he got home.

She supposed it was inevitable that she should be asked if she would accompany him the next morning to see his patient. He had private patients to see at midday and no rounds at the hospital until the afternoon. She got into the car beside him with the dogs nicely settled on the back seat, taking with her a few small luxuries Mevrouw Honig might enjoy, happy to be there beside him. He hadn't said any more about her leaving but it wouldn't be long now, she imagined. Once they had visited Tante Olda he would tell her.

Litrik was pleased with his patient's progress; another few days and she might get up. They drank coffee with Juffrouw de Wit, handed over the odds and ends Fran had brought with her, and drove back. This time there had been no suggestion of going to the pond.

Fran watched Litrik drive off from the house and

went to pay her usual visit to the kitchen and then to Nanny, still industriously plying her needle, and after lunch she telephoned Mevrouw van Rijgen, doubtful about what she should wear to Aunt Olda's party.

'Bring a pretty dress with you, my dear,' counselled Mevrouw van Rijgen. 'It's only family but Tante Olda will expect us to do honour to the occasion. Something short. Litrik tells me you are driving back after the party—a pity you can't stay the night but I expect he had a full day of appointments ahead of him.' There was a faint query in her voice and Fran made haste to say that he was very busy and couldn't manage to get away for more than just the one day. She rang off and went upstairs to go through her wardrobe. She would wear the blue woollen suit and take one of her after-six dresses—the mulberry silk velvet with the long tight sleeves and the satin sash. There were high-heeled velvet slippers to match and perhaps the pearls would be lent to her again.

They left soon after breakfast on Tante Olda's birthday, taking the route through Amsterdam and Hoorn and over the Afsluitdijk so that Fran might see something of that part of Holland. 'For,' as Litrik pointed out blandly, 'you might not have another opportunity to see our famous sea dyke. We'll drive back down the other side of the Isselmeer, but it will be dark then, of course.'

He was at his most interesting pointing out various landmarks which he thought might interest her and never once mentioning the fact that she would be going away very soon. She had hoped, when he had remarked upon her not seeing the Afsluitdijk again, that he would say something about her leaving, but it seemed that it was the last thing he was thinking of.

They stopped for coffee in Alkmaar; it had meant that he had gone into the town expressly for that purpose, but, as he pointed out, they had the time to do so and, like the Afsluitdijk, it was a place it would be a pity for her not to visit while she had the opportunity.

She drank her coffee rather silently, thinking that he seemed determined to remind her that any day now she would be gone, and at the same time he seemed equally determined not to tell her when that was to be.

They arrived at Rinsumaard just before midday, to find a big gathering already there. The aunts lived in a large, rather forbidding house on the edge of the village, it had a large garden around it and its furnishings were opulent and at the same time gloomy. Wilma, greeting Fran in the hall, whispered, 'Isn't it overpowering? All dark oak and family portraits—you ought to see the kitchens. How nice you look. Come and say hallo to the aunts. Tante Olda is having a lovely time...' She turned to Litrik who had been talking to his father. 'Have you bought something fabulous? I've never seen so many handsome presents.' She lifted her face for his kiss. 'Come on, then we can have a drink before lunch.'

Tante Olda received their congratulations and the

brooch with dignity and the command that Fran should return to talk to her later on. 'I rest in the afternoon,' she observed, 'but we must have a little chat before you leave this evening. Such a pity that you have to return tonight; I only hope that Litrik is a careful driver.'

Fran assured her that he was. Very careful but fast, only she didn't say that; she wasn't a very fast driver herself but sitting beside Litrik she enjoyed the exhilarating speed.

She got separated from him after that and during luncheon, since he was sitting at the other end of the vast oval table, she could only get a glimpse of him now and then around the vast floral centrepiece. And after lunch, when the aunts and the elderly had retired for their post-prandial naps, Jebbeke and Wilma carried her off to see the gardens and then explore the house.

'It's like a museum,' said Jebbeke. 'We all hate it, but it's been in the family for years and years and it'll go to Uncle Hilwert, who doesn't want it.'

Fran agreed that it wasn't her idea of a cosy home and thought with sudden longing of Litrik's house, just as big but somehow it was a home, its rooms comfortably furnished, with firelight and lamplight and the dogs lying around and Nel and Tuggs and Nanny. She was going to miss them all—and she was going to miss Litrik for the rest of her life.

'Don't look so sad,' said Wilma, and flung a friendly arm round her shoulders. 'You and Litrik won't have to live here, nor will your children. And aren't you lucky? We are all coming to you at New Year, you know that I expect. We have a lovely time—it's a kind of tradition. When Litrik can tear himself away from his patients you must come and spend a weekend with us.'

Fran wondered what they would think of her when Litrik told them that they had decided to part. He would allow no blame to attach to herself, she know him well enough for that, but all the same she felt guilty.

'You're looking sad again,' said Jebbeke, 'You need a cup of your English tea.' She glanced at her watch. 'It will be in the red salon.'

The red salon was exactly that: red carpet, curtains and upholstery, with a glittering chandelier overhead and stern faced ancestors staring coldly down from the red panelled walls. Several of the family were already there and Litrik crossed the room to join them as they went in.

He included all three of them in his smile, but he spoke to Fran.

'What do you think of the house, Francesca? A little overpowering isn't it? Come over to the fire and have some tea; the aunts aren't coming down until we meet for dinner.'

Tea was a pleasant interlude and presently they scattered again, the men to play billiards, the ladies to enjoy a discussion of the latest fashions, and presently they went upstairs to the various rooms allotted to them to change for the evening.

Fran found herself in a vast room, heavily furnished in the Beidermeyer style with a bathroom and dressing room leading from it. There was no sign of Litrik although his clothes had been laid out in the dressing room. She undressed and had a bath and then dressed quickly in the mulberry velvet. She was sitting at the dressing-table doing things to her face when she heard Litrik in the dressing room, and then presently in the bathroom.

She was quite ready, still sitting at the dressing-table when he tapped on the door and came in. He looked quite splendid in his black tie and her heart turned over at the sight of him and then thumped so loudly that when he came to stand beside her she was afraid that he would hear it.

'A dreadfully depressing room,' remarked Litrik, and added silkily, 'not conducive to connubial bliss.'

She was thinking up a suitable answer to this when he took the pearls out of a pocket and fastened them round her neck. His fingers were cool against her neck and businesslike. He had the earrings, too, and watched while she fastened them, staring at her reflection in the mirror so that she found it difficult to keep her composure.

'Shall we go?' he asked. 'Out of this door, I think—it will look better if we are together, will it not?'

He gave her a brief mocking smile as she went past him.

Everyone had gathered in the drawing room, with Tante Nynke arriving just a few minutes ahead of Tante Olda, who swept in with a fine sense of the dramatic, wearing black satin and a great many diamonds. There were drinks then and a slow procession into the dining room, and this time Fran was between Litrik's cousins, young and only too delighted to entertain her while they ate their way through iced melon, poached salmon, roast pheasant and a magnificent ice pudding, and all of these helped along with champagne. Fran laughed and talked and ate hardly anything, aware of Litrik's eyes upon her face from the other side of the table.

Everyone gathered in the drawing room after dinner, groups forming and dispersing and reforming while Tante Olda sat by the fire in state, talking to first one and then another of the family.

The evening was far gone when Jebbeke tapped Fran on the arm. 'Your turn,' she said lightly. 'Tante Olda wants a chat.'

Litrik had been standing nearby and he had heard his sister. He smiled and nodded at Fran as she crossed the room and sat down beside the old lady, to be looked over by a pair of very shrewd eyes.

'I'm getting tired,' observed Tante Olda, 'but I wanted to talk to you, Francesca; we have had so little opportunity to get to know each other. I do not intend to pry but there are two questions I wish to ask you, and since you are a sensible and honest girl I have no doubt that you will give me truthful answers.'

She was silent for so long that Fran decided that she had dozed off. But she hadn't.

'I am devoted to Litrik—we have always been close, he and I. As a small boy...' She fell silent again and went on in a quite different voice, 'After the disastrous fiasco of his first marriage he changed. Oh, outwardly still charming and an amusing companion, but beneath that, cold and detached, just as though he would never care for anything or anyone again—except for little Lisa, of course. For her, he was his true self. But underneath that coldness there is still the real man, warm and passionate, and you, my dear, are the one to find that man again.' She gave Fran a searching look. 'You do love him, Francesca?'

Fran's heart answered before her sensible head could frame a reply. 'Yes, I love him—I love him so much.'

The old lady nodded in satisfaction. 'You want to have his children?'

'Yes, oh yes, more than anything in the world, but...'

She was interrupted by Litrik's voice behind her. 'Sorry to break up your gossip.' He sounded lazily tolerant. 'I've just noticed the time as I was talking to Father and we really must go—I have a round in the morning.'

Fran had gone pale. How long had he been there and what had he heard?

She glanced quickly at him; his face was calm, his voice casual and his father was standing at the other end of the long room. A stealthy glance told her that Litrik couldn't have had the time to cross the room and overhear what she had said. She heaved a sigh of relief, kissed the elderly proffered cheek, thanked Tante Olda prettily and then accompanied Litrik round the room, saying goodbyes.

It was really goodbye this time, she thought sadly.

Someone had packed their things and fetched the car to the door. She had put her winter coat into the car and now Litrik wrapped her into it and they drove off to a chorus of goodbyes.

It was a cold dark night with frost sparkling on the roof tops and the fields. Litrik drove fast and almost in silence and presently she slept.

The house was warm and welcoming; they drank the coffee Nel had left out before Fran wished Litrik good night. 'I enjoyed it', she ventured a little shyly. 'You do have a nice family, Litrik.'

He gave her a mocking smile. 'Such a pity that you will never get to know them, Francesca. As you have pointed out to me, that is by your own wish.'

There was nothing for her to do but wish him good night for the second time and go up to bed.

She came down to breakfast very late the next morning and he had already gone. She spent an hour with Nel and Nanny, telling them about Tante Olda's party, and then took the dogs for a walk and, because she had slept badly, she dozed in front of the fire after lunch.

Litrik came back at tea time. She sat up as he came into the room and he said pleasantly, 'Catching up on last night's sleep?' He put an envelope on the table beside the chair. 'Your tickets, Francesca. I wasn't able to get you a flight—I've booked you on the night ferry to Harwich for the day after tomorrow.'

She had been expecting it for days and now it had come and she was too taken aback to speak. She picked up the envelope and peered inside. The tickets were there, sure enough, and she said faintly, 'Oh, thank you.'

Litrik sat down in his chair and stretched out his legs, the epitome of relaxed comfort. 'You'll get into London about mid-morning, that gives you plenty of time to go on down to your aunts if you wish, or find an hotel.' He picked up the first of the pile of letters waiting for him. 'I'll see that you have sufficient money and write you a reference—that's what you wanted, isn't it?'

It was a little more than Fran could stand. Illogically she was thunderstruck at the suddenness of it all—she had just one day in which to pack her things and say goodbye to Mevrouw Honig and Dominee Meertens. And what was she to say to the staff?

She said savagely, 'How absolutely beastly of you!'

He lifted his handsome head from the letter he was reading. 'Why, my dear Francesca, you have been badgering me to let you return home for days—I'm surprised at you.'

He lowered his eyes to his letters again and she said in a choked voice, 'Well, I'd better go and start packing.'

When she left the room, Litrik rang for Tuggs and, when that faithful friend came, 'Now listen, Tuggs, there are one or two things I want you to do.' Tuggs listened carefully and went back to the kitchen and when Nel asked him what the doctor had wanted, he told her to ask no questions and she would be told no lies!

Fran, in her room, took a wistful look at the lovely clothes she had bought with Litrik's money, and began to pack the things she had brought with her. She would have to travel in the Jaeger suit for she had no coat with her but she could wear a sweater with it and hope that it wouldn't be too cold a day. Having done this she did her face and hair and went downstairs for dinner, to hold a desultory conversation with Litrik and agree with every appearance of pleasure to his suggestion that, as he intended visiting Mevrouw de Wit in the morning, she might like to go with him.

The old woman was well on the way to recovery, sitting downstairs in a chair by the fire Juffrouw de Wit had kindled in the parlour. She accepted Fran's gift of fruit and biscuits, assured her that she would soon be on her feet once more and asked her if she wanted to go to the pond.

It was after they had all had coffee that Litrik said

that he would like to examine his patient and if Fran wished to go for a stroll perhaps she would like to go now. 'Ten minutes,' he said. 'I must be in Zeist by eleven o'clock.'

So she trod the well-known path once more for the last time and went to sit on the log and watch the coots and listen to the few birds. It had been a happy place with Lisa, but now it was sad; she went back before the ten minutes were up, took a brief farewell of the two ladies and got into the car. Litrik talked cheerfully about his patient during the brief drive back and left at once for the hospital, and she went to the kitchen where she told Nel and Nanny that she would be going to England on the following day. They received her news calmly, hoped that she would have a good time and plunged into the question of whether she wanted all the guestrooms opened and prepared for Christmas. Somehow she escaped answering that and took herself and the dogs for a long walk and directly after lunch went to say goodbye to the *dominee*. She was hurt and surprised at the matter-of-fact manner in which he received her news, and still more disappointed at his vague answers to her anxious questions about the annulment.

'You are anxious to leave us?' he boomed at her.

'Yes—no—that is—I can't explain...' And to her relief he said no more.

Feeling frustrated, she shook hands with him and his wife and as he went down the garden path with her she was perplexed to hear him say, 'Most satisfactory—this is something I had hoped and prayed for.'

She wanted very much to ask him what he meant—he must have been referring to Lisa. She didn't go straight back to the house, but walked on towards the lake, making and discarding plans for her future. She had a little money of her own but she would have to decide quickly where she wanted to go and then look for a job. Litrik had said that he would see that her career wouldn't suffer and she believed him; it would help a lot if she made up her mind before she left the next day, then there would be no need to write to him.

She wandered on, trying to envisage a future without him and filled with despair at the thought. But that was a waste of time and the sooner she stopped mooning after him, she told herself briskly, the better. She would tell him that she would like to work in Scotland; she wasn't fussy where but preferably in a large hospital where there was plenty of work. Her mind made up, she turned for home, pecked at her lunch and went to her room to finish her packing. That done, she spent half an hour fingering the lovely things still hanging in the closet, wondering what Litrik would do about them. They were too small for Nanny, and his sisters were big girls. Besides, they had more than enough money to buy anything they wanted. It was a pity she must leave the winter coat, it would have been a comfort on the journey.

Litrik didn't come home for tea and although he

came in just before dinner, he went out again almost immediately they had finished. She sat in the drawing room knitting, her mind refusing to think any more.

He was at breakfast, wishing her good morning as usual and, before he went to the hospital, warning her to be ready to leave at eight o'clock that evening. 'I shall be back by six o'clock so will you arrange dinner for an hour earlier than usual—we can leave directly after that.'

'We?' asked Fran startled. She had expected Tuggs to drive her to Utrecht to catch the boat train.

'Naturally I shall drive you myself.'

He had gone, leaving her to spend her last day roaming round the house and the gardens. At least she would have the chance to talk to him about her plans, for the drive to the Hoek would take an hour, perhaps more. She had herself nicely in hand by the time he returned in the evening, made rather feverish small talk during dinner, said goodbye to everyone and got into the Daimler. It was a brilliant night, the wind still and with a silver moon giving sparkle to the frost, and there was not much traffic. She settled down beside Litrik and began to compose the various questions in her head. They had skirted Utrecht before she had them exactly as she wished and then she forgot every one of them as they passed a road sign.

'We're going the wrong way,' she said urgently. 'Emmeloord and Leeuwarden—the Hoek's the other way.'

'We are not going to the Hoek,' said Litrik calmly.

'I'm going to miss the boat... Why not?' She took a steadying breath. 'Where are we going?'

'To a cottage I have near Sneek.' He gave a great sigh. 'You see, my dear, I am in love with you and I cannot let you go.'

The road was straight and empty before them; he slowed the car and stopped. 'I believe that I have loved you for a long time now, perhaps since that first time when I made you cry during that lecture—afterwards I felt as though I had wounded some small creature and left it to die. Then I met you again and I knew that you were exactly the mother Lisa had wished for for so long—a mouse, she had said, and that is what you are, a small beautiful mouse with a soft voice and lovely eyes and a gentle mouth and I knew for certain then that I loved you. Only you had made it clear that for you our marriage was purely for Lisa's sake and I have tried very hard to keep to my side of our pact.'

Fran stirred in her seat. 'Could we get out?' she asked softly. 'Please?'

He went round the car and took something from the boot and opened her door and she saw that he had her coat over his arm.

'I went to look in your room—I guessed what you would do. You see how well I know you, my darling? I asked Nel to pack some of your things and put this into the car.'

He helped her into it and buttoned it up cosily under her chin and took her arm and began walking along the road. Fran looked into his face, very clear in the moonlight. 'I love you,' she said, 'but how did you know? Because you do know, don't you?' She frowned. 'You heard me and Tante Olda?'

'I eavesdropped quite shamelessly, my darling, reminding myself that all is fair in love and war. You see, I know Tante Olda very well indeed; she has this habit of asking searching questions. I know you, too, and I knew you would answer her honestly.'

'You could have told me on our way home.'

'You slept, my love. And I wanted to be sure— that's why I gave you the tickets. And you seemed pleased so that I wanted to hurt you.'

'Well, you did,' declared Fran, 'and I really can't think why I love you so very much for sometimes you are so tiresome.'

He stopped and swung her round into his arms and let out a great bellow of laughter. 'Oh, I will try so hard not to be tiresome,' he promised her and kissed her gently and then very hard and indeed, and presently he took her arm again and began walking back to the car. And as they went he stopped to kiss her once in a while. 'Love in the moonlight,' he observed, 'there is nothing quite like it.'

'Tell me,' said Fran, 'this cottage—are we going to stay there?'

'For a week—Mama's retired cook lives there and looks after it for me; Tuggs will have phoned her and told her to expect us.'

'Supposing that I had insisted on going to the Hoek?'

'I should have kidnapped you,' said Litrik, and kissed her once again.

eHARLEQUIN.com

Becoming an eHarlequin.com member is easy, fun and **FREE!** Join today to enjoy great benefits:

- **Super savings** on all our books, including members-only discounts and offers!

- Enjoy **exclusive online reads**—FREE!

- Info, tips and **expert advice** on writing your own romance novel.

- FREE romance **newsletters,** customized by you!

- Find out the latest on your **favorite authors.**

- Enter to win exciting **contests and promotions!**

- Chat with other members in our **community message boards!**

Plus, we'll send you 2 FREE Internet-exclusive eHarlequin.com books (no strings!) just to say thanks for joining us online.

——— To become a member, ———
visit www.eHarlequin.com today!

If you enjoyed what you just read,
then we've got an offer you can't resist!

Take 2 bestselling
love stories FREE!
Plus get a FREE surprise gift!

Clip this page and mail it to Harlequin Reader Service®

IN U.S.A.
3010 Walden Ave.
P.O. Box 1867
Buffalo, N.Y. 14240-1867

IN CANADA
P.O. Box 609
Fort Erie, Ontario
L2A 5X3

YES! Please send me 2 free Harlequin Romance® novels and my free surprise gift. After receiving them, if I don't wish to receive anymore, I can return the shipping statement marked cancel. If I don't cancel, I will receive 6 brand-new novels every month, before they're available in stores! In the U.S.A., bill me at the bargain price of $3.34 plus 25¢ shipping & handling per book and applicable sales tax, if any*. In Canada, bill me at the bargain price of $3.80 plus 25¢ shipping & handling per book and applicable taxes**. That's the complete price and a savings of 10% off the cover prices—what a great deal! I understand that accepting the 2 free books and gift places me under no obligation ever to buy any books. I can always return a shipment and cancel at any time. Even if I never buy another book from Harlequin, the 2 free books and gift are mine to keep forever.

186 HDN DNTX
386 HDN DNTY

Name	(PLEASE PRINT)	
Address	Apt.#	
City	State/Prov.	Zip/Postal Code

 * Terms and prices subject to change without notice. Sales tax applicable in N.Y.
** Canadian residents will be charged applicable provincial taxes and GST.
   All orders subject to approval. Offer limited to one per household and not valid to
   current Harlequin Romance® subscribers.
   ® are registered trademarks of Harlequin Enterprises Limited.

HROM02   ©2001 Harlequin Enterprises Limited

Welcome to Cooper's Corner...
a small town with very big surprises!

Coming in April 2003...
JUST ONE LOOK
by Joanna Wayne

Check-in: After a lifetime of teasing, Cooper's Corner postmistress Alison Fairchild finally had the cutest nose ever—thanks to recent plastic surgery! At her friend's wedding, all eyes were on her, except those of the gorgeous stranger in the dark glasses—then she realized he was blind.

Checkout: Ethan Granger wasn't the sightless teacher everyone thought, but an undercover FBI agent. When he met Alison, he was thankful for those dark glasses. If she could see into his eyes, she'd know he was in love....

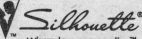